I0684458

LUCY

Alan Kennedy

LASSERRADE

Copyright © Alan Kennedy 2014

ISBN 978-0-9564696-6-3

Alan Kennedy has asserted his right under the Copyright Designs and Patents Act 1988 to be identified as the author of this work

First published in the United Kingdom in 2014 by Lasserrade Press.

By the same author:

The Boat in the Bay, Lasserrade Press, 2010

The Broken Bell, Lasserrade Press, 2011

The Pink House, Lasserrade Press, 2013

For EWK

Peindre d'abord une cage

CHAPTER 1

There had been two letters waiting for her when she got back that day: May the eighth, 1945. They called it VE Day for Victory in Europe. It was in the newspaper, although Lucy was sure it would never catch on. It sounded vainglorious somehow. Anyway, wars don't end, do they? This one didn't. It just seemed to peter out, leaving everybody exhausted. Who the hell felt victorious? The word was ridiculous. She'd seen the letters lying there when she got in. It seemed like all day she'd been walking - just to get over the shock of things; to get things straight in her head. Dundee had managed a little spring sunshine for the victory. Across Balgay Hill, through the graveyard, then down onto Magdalen Green, meeting the raw wind off the Tay. She had stood looking at the bandstand, thinking she should go home. Some men had climbed up and were acting the goat, marching round and round, playing *Come to the Cookhouse door boys* on bugles. They seemed no more than boys themselves, barely into double figures. A little knot of women stood watching. Some were smiling, but not all of them. If you walk back along the Perth Road you see chestnut trees, not yet filled with snowy candles, not yet quite in leaf; trees are late in Dundee. No traffic either, not for VE Day. You could walk down the middle of an empty road if you wanted. As if you were going nowhere at all.

The letters were on the little table in the hall. There was surely no post today? Not on VE Day? The girl who came to clear up must have brought them. Lucy spread them out. One was typed, with that pretentious blue eagle on the back. Hilary. God knows why she thought an embossed eagle did something; she must have got them as a job lot. Before the war, because you couldn't get paper like that now. Thick stuff. No, you couldn't fault the paper. The other letter was square. A funny shape, square. Not business, so pleasure. Could you say pleasure? And lots inside, because it was positively bulging. Blue ink, a firm confident hand, the letters square like the envelope. Across the top a spidery pencil had put, *Try N° 6*, which seemed odd at first because the address was clear enough. Then you saw the problem was the name: this one said "Poppy". Although that was right in a way: Poppy was right enough. It was just that Poppy had stopped; was no more. Stopped years back.

She took the letters into the living room, flopping down on the sofa and kicking her shoes off. There was nothing on the back of the square one, which was a disappointment. You couldn't read the post office stamp either. Just a black smudge. Nothing for it really, but to open the damned thing. But "Poppy"? Now she thought about it, she didn't like that, didn't like it one bit. Who'd go digging her up after all this time? No good would come of it, that's for sure. No, Poppy would have to wait her turn.

She broke open the other envelope, the embossed eagle snapping away clean. There was a single sheet inside: thick, pale blue, with *Edinburgh Fine Art* in tiny Gothic script on a single line across the top. Absurdly small letters, confident of the vanity of advertisement. It was an invoice.

There was nothing much to read apart from, "To framing etc" set out in a rather pompous style between thin vertical lines, the sum typed in red. It hardly made sense. Of course, there were always accounts, setting out receipts, less this and that. Only it appeared this time it was for Lucy to pay. She had vaguely expected it, but not now, with that disaster of a show not even closed.

There was something scrawled unevenly across the bottom in Hilary's special baby writing. She could barely read it, thick green ink spraying out from its expensive nib. She took the page to the window and held it there, tipping it back into the soft evening light.

Sorry Sorry Sorry – the paintings were lovely. They always are. People are so stupid. You must come by and we'll have a natter about old times. You remember Saint-Valery? I do. I always will. Kisses. Hilly.

Lucy stood for a good long time staring sightlessly down into the street below, holding the sheet of paper, surprised at how little she felt. She had often wondered how it would all start to unravel; how the humiliation would happen. And the answer was with kisses. The same as with Jesus. No, that wasn't fair: you couldn't blame the woman. Last Saturday in the gallery had been a nightmare. Neat lines of glinting glasses a reproach to the empty room. It had been a mistake to fill them. She remembered thinking perhaps you could pour it all back. It looked too cold somehow. Could you drink red wine that cold?

The place was freezing. Don't expect Edinburgh nights to be warm in May, not with that cutting wind. A stove somewhere downstairs had given up and Hilary had carried an electric fire through, its ineffective little glow making things worse. People kept their overcoats on - both people, to be precise. A couple whispering together, not daring to look at the walls. They seemed embarrassed, awkward, wondering why they'd come; and soon enough they were scuttling shiftily into the night, only turning back for a second to make a fuss pulling the door to, as if that made everything alright. All the while Hilary talking, talking, talking, until Lucy could have brained her. Endlessly talking, eyes nervily flicking to the street door at every passing shadow. Not that many shadows passed here. You don't get passing traffic in the New Town. People have to decide to come; have to bother to make the effort. And it seemed they hadn't.

The gallery stood empty for an hour before a crowd arrived, the fag end of some party from a restaurant by the Castle. They'd seen the lights and the wine and crowded in like so many well-lubricated penguins. Lucy had stood against the wall with frozen hands and a frozen smile, watching as one or two glanced idly at the pictures, perhaps wondering why there were so many on the walls. She decided to run away as Hilary began pushing between these strangers, hopelessly looking for a face she might know, her head bobbing among the black waves, drowning. As Lucy pushed past, Hilary tugged pointlessly at her sleeve, desperate, lost. A tight little smile was all she could manage back, already feeling sick with the taste of the wine. It was the cigar smell that did it, reminding you too much of Albert, and Albert wasn't here; wouldn't be coming, that was for sure. She fought a way through to the door and stumbled out onto the stones of the pavement, the raw of the air catching her throat.

It was virtually black outside, just the bleak halo of a faint gas lamp higher up the street, everywhere silent, horribly cold, you would think a frost was starting. The telephone rang as she turned to close the door. She saw Hilary holding the receiver out, waving it as if to show something to some invisible person on the other end, shouting to make herself heard above the silence. You had to admit she tried, did Hilary. It must have been that man from the newspaper. Martin Keynes, the *Manchester Guardian* man. He'd been yesterday while they were still hanging the show and declared himself bowled over, but people say things like that, don't they? He'd told Hilary he'd be at the opening *without fail*; then again, people say things. Perhaps he did come after all, arriving fashionably late. She'd done the same herself often enough. But it would be red spots he'd be counting, and when Lucy left they had added up to precisely none. Perhaps he could write that in his review: a spotless show, certainly scope for a bit of coffin humour there.

There was the other letter: the blue ink one, the bulging one. Time was she would have tossed a letter like that in the air and let it fall into Albert's lap giving him her pretend shocked look. And he would have shouted back, "Not your secret admirer?" and they would both laugh. He had written before: rambling letters of adoration. Illustrated, what's more; you had to admit the chap had a certain perverse talent with ink. Not always completely delicate, but harmless enough. The price of fame, Albert would say, lighting another cigar. You had to put up with anonymous admirers, not that he had any, you have to be a woman to get those. And he would pretend to be put out. But it had been true, certainly true – she was famous. No, she had better say, had been famous. *Had been* – that was more like it.

"Poppy," the letter said. Like something she ought to remember. A faint echo claiming her for what she had been. A reproach if you like, because, truth to tell, she had been happy enough with Poppy. Mother sitting in her chair, talking to Daddy as if he hadn't died, as if he was still there. When Mother was like that she always said Poppy. Fumbling with that little book of photographs as if that was him. Four or five unfocussed fragments of all his time. The best one, head up, wide-eyed, a fork raised to his lips, grinning and looking past the camera, past you, at something you couldn't see. Or somebody. You'll never know. That was what war did, they said, as if that explained it. The lottery of life: today you live and eat and raise your fork; tomorrow the bomb falls. Tomorrow you stop. Only it wasn't a bomb, it was a heart attack. So not a bomb, just the relentless nagging fear of a bomb; much the same really.

She had offered to paint him for Mother. She knew she could have managed something, even something good. But Mother only shook her head. It was a nice thought, but not now he'd gone; anyway, she'd never really understood that sort of painting, so better not.

Lucy felt the letter lying heavy in her hand. She must have picked it up without noticing. Who would write to her here? *Who?* was bad enough, but *Why?* was worse. Lucy knew all about *Why?* – and it was always worse. It was getting dark. The light was good for painting here, evenly from the North. Sunlight came second-hand reflected from window panes on the other side. There was a view, but you would have to live outside to see it. A perverse geometry applied to this part of Dundee. Higher up, broad streets ran parallel with a river wide as the sea, but the houses here ran down to meet the Tay, with nothing to look at across the cliff of space but each other. It was already getting dark. She lit the gas and slumped back into her place, letting the anaesthetic hiss settle into her brain. It was a yellow light. You couldn't paint in a yellow light. Maybe that didn't matter anymore. Not after Spotless Saturday. She'd have something to eat and then read it.

The girl had left a cold supper in the kitchen: corned beef, thin slices of onion, soaked to take the taste away, a few limp pieces of beetroot wet with vinegar, half a loaf of bread. She had filled a glass jug with water and left bottled beer on the sideboard. You could do worse on a damp Tuesday in Dundee. Bonny, they called it and sometimes that seemed right. Although not Peddie Street; you couldn't really call Peddie Street bonny. The bread tasted of war: a stale under-taste, something just short of mould breaking through the scrape of butter. You soon got used to it. She opened the beer, settled down, and tore open the envelope.

My dear Poppy

I can't say how many times I've started this letter, but you know I was never one for writing things down. After that awful day. And we both said such things! Well, I know I did. I never meant one word of it. Not a word, honest. But

then you were gone and I felt so lost. Floods of tears …
And where were you? The exchange said you didn't have a
telephone number. I would never have known how easy it
is just to disappear. You vanished. So if you do get this, it's
to say sorry …

That word again: Hilary's word. How the English do love to say sorry. It was to be the mot du jour – two in one jour, in fact. Sorry makes everything alright. She rifled through the bundle of pages. What a lot of it there was. Could she read all that? Did she want to after all she'd been through today? She really didn't need to look, but the signature was on the last page. That same square writing: 'Elizabeth'. Then, 'Bradley' in afterthought brackets, almost as an apology. A little bleat of do you remember me?

Elizabeth. It really had been years and years. When they were children, playing together. The days of Poppy, before Lucy even existed. She must have been eleven or so. Elizabeth had been older than all of them, but not that much. How old now? She must be in her thirties. Widowed and thirty plus: what could be worse than that? Well, what about thirty and never married. Ever likely to be? Well. That was a question, wasn't it?

Did she really want to read all this? How people hang on to the past. They must have had a quarrel. What had all that been about? She struggled to remember, but nothing would come. Nothing but fugitive glimpses of golden summers a life ago. And for a fleeting second a sweet ache of unbearable nostalgia filled her heart.

… so if you get this it's to say sorry for my part.

After Stuart I just couldn't cope. Of course he was your
brother, so you know. How badly I'm putting this. But he
was that to me as well – that and so much more. And we
were so happy – I'm sure we were. He was my whole life
you know. Still is, if the truth's to be told.

I wonder whether I'll post this or tear it up like the others? This time I've made up my mind. I'll finish and send it, honest.

I didn't know where you were. Even now I don't know for sure. I wheedled it out of somebody at a gallery. In New Bond Street. You must know it. Lots of places bombed on the other side, but this was alright, apart from one window. I won't say who he was because he said he mustn't tell. But you know me, I can wheedle for England. I got it out of him. Don't blame him – it was seeing a picture in the window, the other window, not the broken one. It was a miracle seeing it although it wasn't your name – I suppose artists do that. But I knew it was yours straight away. It reminded me of the Pink House, all muddled up. He wasn't going to tell me the address, but I went at it.

After I lost Stuart I thought I'd die as well. I think I did die. Something got taken out of me. I manage well enough, but with only half of me there. The rest went with him – wherever he is, the dear boy. And I miss him every day. Laura knows that. She's a warrior you know. She told me she couldn't cope at all when she heard. I'd never understood sisters and brothers stuff, there just being me at home, but Laura said it was like losing a bit of herself, a big bit. I suppose it's being the same flesh, if you think about it. Laura's happy enough to live with half a girl. She loves me. She says she does and I really believe her because I can't give her much back for it. We've been that way since Stuart went. She came here one afternoon. Just walked down from the station. It must have been six months after. And now I suppose we shall be like this for ever. I know it all sounds very queer, but it suits us.

I wrote to Ian and tried to explain. He was really splendid about it. He sent some hideously expensive flowers and a card with "Now I have a new sister. Very modern! Bravo!" on it. For all the world like a wreath, Laura said, held together with wire. It was sweet of him, although I suppose it was all done by one of his army of little helpers. Some smart girl must have ordered them over the telephone. Laura said they would have done well for a funeral. We laughed about it. He's still in Paris I think. Or is it Brussels? Somewhere important, anyway. The usual hush hush Ian. I wrote to him pleading for your address but there was no reply and I was so upset I cried, but I realise now he didn't know. He must have thought he should know, being your brother, and wouldn't admit he didn't. Just like him.

What a bore this letter is – just a list of people. I don't even know whether you remember. Whether you want to know ...

Lucy realised her hand was unsteady. Why was it doing that? Surely she wasn't going to land up with trembling hands, was she? Not hanging on to a maulstick like the ancient Renoir? It was right what they said - the past didn't go away. It invaded you, entered you, remade you. It ate you. She looked dispassionately down at the fingers of her right hand, remembering how once she had tried to draw them with the left, just to see if she could. The tips were trembling. So her fingers knew, even if she didn't. No, Elizabeth, you're wrong about Ian. He had the address – he just wasn't going to tell. But I do want to know. How I want to know. God, you won't believe how much I want to know.

She pulled the bunched pages apart, hurriedly passing them from hand to hand, scanning page after page of ink. There were names, but not the one that mattered. Not a mention of his name. Poor Elizabeth – never quite getting the right end of the stick.

Poppy dear, I'll tell you why I'm writing. It's about Uncle Albert. It's you they should have written to, I know, but I'm 'blood' they say. How weird the French are, always going on about blood. All those years you spent there. I never understood about painting, you know that. At least not the way you and Uncle A went at it – burning yourselves up.

Mum couldn't forgive him staying in France. She was very bitter about it: him in his Pink House entertaining the awful Hun, she'd say. Supping with the devil. They fell out over it most dreadfully. He didn't come to her funeral. But you know that, of course, because you couldn't, could you? Stuck there with the war going on. Anyway, they say with dad dead, I'm the only one left that counts as blood. So they wrote to me.

It was more than a week ago. That was why I was so desperate to find you. I got this great cardboard parcel from lawyers in Paris. There's envelopes inside for all of us. Uncle has found a lawyer who can write something in a sort of English, I wouldn't have made much of it otherwise. I don't know why he won't write himself. Well, I do know I suppose. It's him falling out with Mother. Family squabbles. The lawyer says he had tried to get Ian's address and asked at the Embassy in Paris. I suppose he wanted a man to write to – they usually do. Anyway, they wouldn't say, apart from send it to them. He couldn't do that so he had to swallow his pride and send it to me. I got all of it in a big parcel. Covered in red stamps. I'd forgotten how the French love their stamps. And yards of red ribbon inside. Remember how we used to play with red ribbons? It brought it all back. They're just the same.

The papers for the island are in the packet – pages and pages of stuff in handwriting. And a plan. It's got a name – but you must know that. There's "Malapet" written down the middle in old-fashioned curly handwriting, so I suppose that's the name. It sounds a bit sinister. There's something in an envelope with Stuart's name on it, but I couldn't read it – too upsetting anyway. Apparently Uncle's told them to write saying what's to happen when he's dead. He wants me to have the house when he dies - the Pink House. It hardly seems right, with you living there all that time. And there's dozens of paintings, all listed with titles and sizes and everything. And land. I never realised – he owns all those forests, miles and miles. There's a plan of it all, in little parcels, hundreds of them.

There's a letter, well a note really. Just a scribble. You know the way he is when he's cross. He sounds cross. It just says "Elizabeth, you'll have to come if you want to get this straight. I'm too old." So what do I do? The lawyer says he's at our disposal, but I'm not sure what that means. Apparently I can sign something and he does things on my behalf, but I suppose that would be an end to it really. It all seems so far away. There's something about money as well. There's a lot of money to see to apparently. But his English got so bad at that point I could barely make it out. I suppose it means he wants his claw on it. Lawyers are like that. Perhaps that's unfair – I don't know.

Hello again Poppy. I just went and lay down. Had a good cry. I do that when Laura's out. She never says anything. I sometimes wish she would. She's doing the flowers in the church. It's been so bloody writing all this and thinking about us and Uncle and the island and all that. Do you remember camping? And the scrapes we got into? It all seems such a long time ago. This war has blighted everything.

I'm going to wait two weeks and see whether you reply. I think I ought to go and see him. Will you come with me? Please say yes. If you can't, I'll sign the little man's form and that's that. I really don't know he's little – I just imagine him that way.

Poppy dear, do write and tell me what I should do. I always used to know what to do, but not since Stuart's gone. You're part of him.

I won't read it through. I bet it's an awful muddle.

    Elizabeth

The light in the room seemed suddenly too bright, the curtains still drawn back against the black. There was a horse outside, slowly pulling its way up the hill to the top of the Blackness Road, turning across to the park. It was very late for delivering anything. He must be going home. The clop clop and the slow grate of iron wheels reminded her of something vaguely comforting.

CHAPTER 2

Quite a shock to see *Malapet* – she'd never seen it written down before. It had been years since she'd thought about the place, although when they were children she had thought of little else. Dear old Uncle Albert, carrying a torch for a girl all those years, a girl he never had, a girl who died. Death can stalk you like that if you're not careful, run up behind you and drag at you for the rest of your life. Uncle Albert, finding solace in being unbelievably kind to other people's children, having none of his own. *Malapet*, their own little island, the place he gave them to propitiate his gods, or his demons, when he might have lost his own life. And that was true enough – if it hadn't been for them he would be dead now. But he wasn't, it was Stuart who had gone. Stuart come to dust, like the poor chimney sweepers. How could they possibly have guessed that in those golden days? On the other hand, what did giving away his precious island really cost Albert? Nothing at all, because he was impossibly rich. Still is, if it comes to it, even in his disgraceful exile. Or perhaps *because* of his disgraceful exile. People queued to snap up whatever he painted. Whatever *he* put on canvas sold. No, that was unfair; no point being bitter. All the same, it had been a curious gift to a bunch of children in a country like France where land and blood were inseparable. She supposed you could get French lawyers to do anything if you paid them enough, but there were bound to be problems in the end, and here they were, arriving on cue in Elizabeth's square ink.

Lucy poured out the remains of the beer and took the glass into the living room. Did she want to see Elizabeth? Did she want to go back to the Pink House? Not exactly a place of golden memories for her, even if Elizabeth was filled with nostalgic fervour. Wasn't it a golden rule never to go back? If she went now it would be breaking it in spades. There was a cloud over France. Two clouds, if she told the truth. When was it that carefree France became ever so slightly less carefree? When was the first cloud? There must have been a moment, but she couldn't remember; hard to put your finger on it. When was it that giving it a miss *just for that year*, shaded into never going back at all? When was it that breathless preparations for the annual Pink House holiday became less pressing? There must have been a point when Mother had said perhaps not, but exactly when was unclear. You only really hold on to sharp things and the change had been too gradual to recall: an imperceptible shift in orientation that defeated her. Then she remembered - it had started with Vienna. It must have been a few years before the war. She remembered Father saying Christmas was just as much fun in London. He made it a jolly thing to say, but she had sensed unease in the room, sensed even then there was more to it, more than the discomfort of over-heated continental trains. After that, there was no Austria anymore, and certainly no Germany. Too complicated for the children to understand, it was left that holidays were best at home. So *Malapet* became just a memory. For the others, a place of wistful summer dreams. For her? Well, that would be telling wouldn't it? That would be the second cloud. And she couldn't explain that because it still hurt too much.

Elizabeth was wrong about one thing. There was nothing sinister at all about the name; it was just a tribute to scorching sand. Too hot in summer to risk bare feet. The first visitors to that island had been masons, crossing the strait in rowboats loaded with blocks of stone for the watch tower. Hundreds of years ago. They must have cursed the place, *mal aux pieds*, and the name stuck. It was funny, in all those holidays they'd never visited that tower; planned to go many a time, but never quite got there. The closest was that day she first saw Oscar.

And as the name came to her, Lucy looked across the room, conscious of mist blurring the globe of the lamp. Just mist, no more than that; she wasn't going to weep. No more crying on your own, those days were long over. Although you had to admit that distant day had been worth a quiet sob or two: the day she first saw Oscar. The day that settled her life for good. The day that put her on the same path as Albert. If they'd not set off on the trek to the watch tower that day she would never have met Oscar and everything would have been different. Absolutely everything: every second of her whole existence.

When is it not like that? Life's little forking paths: *this way favours lie, that way despair* – that's the measure of it. You just have to get on with it, not think about the other paths too much. She could do that because regrets were not worth painting, and painting was all that mattered. All that mattered for Albert as well. The frightening thing is, you never see the forks until you look back. Who was it wrote about the choice of roads, *Sorry I could not travel both*? Stupid, stupid, stupid. Sentimental and stupid, trying to have it both ways, a cheap way to trick you out of regrets. No, mister poet, whoever you were, you only get to feel sorry afterwards: that's the big lesson. That's Lucy's First Law and you'd better know it. You can't properly be sorry until it's too late. She always thought that too late stuff was one of God's best jokes; in her life, anyway. Because if anybody wanted a potted summary of Lucy (although after that show last Saturday it would appear few did), too late would do fine.

The gas had started to flutter against the mantle, spurting gold. You only noticed that when it was really quiet. It was quiet now. Just the hiss and that sweet half-burnt smell like a headache coming on. Lucy tidied the pages of the letter and put them neatly on the table. Nothing wrong with being neat, after all. Perhaps that was what had been wrong with the paintings: too neat. Or not neat enough. It was a disappointment, no getting away from it. How long had she spent on them? It must be two years. Hard to credit it – two years in this place. After France, Dundee had seemed brutish beyond belief. Even now, she was pressed to find anything soft to lean on. Two years painting in cold brittle light that forgave nothing: it had seemed a torment. Perhaps God really did forsake places, in which case Dundee was on the list.

Hilary had suggested nineteen paintings, an awkward sort of number, but in the end she found things did not stop at nineteen. How could she have anticipated that? The last two painted themselves. So it had been twenty-one. The best things she had ever done, she was sure of it. Painting them had hurt more than she had thought possible, because of Oscar. She would never want to feel like that again.

It was dark outside now. For a few minutes the sky over the Law hill had been filled with silent rockets splintering into cascades of stars, green and red. She remembered the Victory. They were probably dancing somewhere. She went into the kitchen and filled a kettle. Time for the cup that cheers. A fierce burst of something like rage suddenly invaded her. Damn Hilary! Damn her pretentious invoice! Damn the lot of them! She had known from the day she started they were worth something – worth the looking; worth her life. God knows what it cost her. Once the state beyond exhaustion arrived you weren't painting at all; just looking right through the canvas. Only once before in her life had she known that feeling. Looking right out the other side, where all that really matters is. And she'd been there for days on end, standing until the fierce pain in her legs was as much a part of the painting as the sick hollow in her heart.

Forgetting to eat. Forgetting to be. She'd never understood what people meant when they talked about a state of grace; it must be what they meant. Those last two had been right; those last two had come almost where she wanted. She looked at them and her heart knew they were right. Oscar would have known as well. She had looked and wondered who the hell painted them.

The whistle on the kettle had started to wheeze – all it could ever manage – and Lucy filled a mug, stirring in goo from the bottle. Coffee was quicker than tea. Camp Coffee it said. Well, whoever thought of that had never been near a camp. For a sweet fleeting second she saw Laura, bent over her circle of stones, holding a match to dry moss. How did she manage that? It was always just the one match and the fire would be away. Dear old Laura – more of a mother than a sister – always bossing them about. She slumped back in the chair letting the acid stuff trickle down her throat. At least it was hot. That's what Mother always said: "At least it's hot". Daddy lying on his back in the hospital bed, the sheets too tight across his chest. Tucked in. It was all they could do really, make him look neat. Neatness is something, after all. Mother managing a dreadful sort of smile, practising being brave. And she always added, "But I suppose we shouldn't complain". Nobody had told Hilary she shouldn't complain.

Funny to think the pictures had risked their way to Edinburgh before this idiot Victory Day. We were still at war; you don't get told when it's going to end. Even then, bombs could have rained down on unsuspecting Kirkaldy as the train puffed through, casual explosion still being a necessary part of life. That was what war did - license things to explode. Cars would explode and the very thought of that would break your heart. But the van with its twenty-one boxes had rattled intact out of the College yard and later she followed them, catching a train from Tay Bridge station, uniforms jostling everywhere, her compartment inexplicably full of Poles.

She had watched Hilary walk along where the paintings had been propped against the walls. Somebody had left an unfortunate bowl of lilies on a table, a relic of some other show. They were dying and the gallery smelled like a funeral. Hilary clacked about, the wooden floors echoing like an empty church. She explained she was *marking out*. Hilary with her bloody little notebook and dripping pen. She reached the last two and stopped for long silent minutes, looking down with a pretend frown, tapping the book with the end of her pen.

'I thought we'd said nineteen. I'm sure the contract said nineteen, didn't it?' Not really a question, just keeping her in her place; letting her know the gallery was going up in the world. For God's sake, there was room enough on the walls: the place was empty. Hilary slyly pulled out the magic two and propped them by her own chair.

'We'll want these in though, won't we? But you see they are so big ... let me look.' Greedy little eyes sizing up. She flashed her best smile. 'I know what we can do. Keep these and take out two of the others. To keep the number right ...' A tinkling little laugh. 'These two do come off awfully well.'

Leave her to stammer herself to a halt, one hand stretched out towards her booty; she was going to get no help. Lucy shrugged, pulled brown paper over them and stacked them by the door. If she doesn't want them all, she won't get them all. Hilary conceded with a little frown. You had to feel sorry for her, poor little Hilary, messing about with painting, pretending it wasn't the money because she was different: she was Hilary; she cared. But it was always the money, wasn't it, my dear? That's what paid for the blue eagles and the fat paper. Although when you came to think about it there could hardly be a worse way of making money: selling other people's souls. Pimping for Apollo somebody called it. That was about right. For no reason at all she suddenly remembered that last show of Albert's, at the Pink House, before the war. Those days a few telephone calls and dealers rolled up in droves. She'd painted that scene after his show, the last of the sun dipping over the lawn, relaxing the heat. Everywhere pink and blue, little cane tables, their feet bedded into the damp grass; plates under white lace covers; tall glasses.

And Albert in his straw hat, legs stretched out, lighting a little cigar. You couldn't really see dealers picking their way down Peddie Street, could you? Not climbing the stone stairs, even if the gas lit the way – which it didn't. No, not really. Dundee was a bad place to be, right enough.

Did she want to see Elizabeth again? The last page of her letter lay on the sofa. Did she want to see a changed Laura? And Stuart - did she want to see him? Not fair, because Stuart was dead. Impossible to think she'd not see him again. Even if she never saw any of them again, everything was different because Stuart really was lost. Lost, along with the only person who had ever made sense.

When exactly had she seen Stuart last? She tried to remember, but it wouldn't come. It seemed unfair; there was no memory at all. Then again, they had not known it was to be goodbye: nothing in all the forking paths of Stuart led him to say this is the last time you'll see me, look your best. She let the tears start into her eyes. What did you call them? Crocodile tears. False tears. Because, love Stuart as she did, the tears were not for him. These were tears for quite another. Isn't that what they do with gravestones? Squeeze in a name like an afterthought: *And Emily, his beloved wife*; something like that. She let the tears fall. Tears for a lost boy long ago. A boy with crinkly hair, almost like a girl's.

CHAPTER 3

Before they went home from the Pink House that last year she had begged a photograph off Uncle Albert, daring him with her boldest look to ask her why. She must have been about twelve, made a little brazen by the fever of first love, waiting till bedtime to cut Oscar out, hiding him in her sketch book. A little clip of card to gauge the day she would reach his age. The day she would be tall enough to stand at ease next to the boy with the crinkly hair. Although, truth to tell, the sepia blur reaching up to gather fruit from a tree could have been almost anybody.

She had not much wanted to go with them on the trek to the tower that particular day; you couldn't call it fun trudging over the insufferable sands of *Malapet*. Albert had brought them across in his boat to set his big easel up on the landing stage and she would have been more than content to sit at his side and watch. But even Albert must have craved the odd day off. Put-upon Uncle Albert, wanting a day to himself, free from children, stuffing things inexpertly into knapsacks, shamelessly passing them to Laura to get straight. Mumbling to himself, not so very quietly, for her to make her mind up: was she going or not? A look of exasperation on his face, stumping off without her, pausing only to toss a water bottle onto the sand at her feet.

But that was the walk that changed her life, all the same: you can never tell. She had got herself to the back of the line snaking its way along the margin of the shore, watching Ian sneaking his shoes off, tying the laces together to hang them round his neck. Ian, no longer the obedient little brother, edging into deeper and deeper water, jumping back in time as the swell rose cold against his legs, daring Laura or Stuart to call out. Those days it was easy for little Iggie to be happy.

They'd been delivered the sort of morning you only got on *Malapet* - crystal light like nowhere else. An immense watery sky rearing over dark banks of trees; a breeze, sharp and fresh off the sea; everywhere the sweet rotten smell of seaweed. Nobody had wanted to talk, not even Ian; it had been like that all morning. As if they were waiting for something; as if they knew.

God knows why she stopped, but she did. Only for a minute, letting the others walk on, slipping her sandals off, feeling soft ridged sand give between her toes, a breeze low off the water flapping at her shirt, the cold shiver of it against her body oddly exciting. Looking out to the horizon, her mind filled with a strange sense of elevation, mesmerised by a swirling silky surface of swell: blue on white, white on blue, creamy foam rising warm against her legs. The sight of it scalded her. Nobody could have painted that, not even a part of it. All those galleries of painted seascapes seemed suddenly so much wasted spirit. It was pointless even looking. Endless gradations of shifting sea stunning you; defeating you.

How long had she stood there? It seemed an eternity. An iridescent mass of water listlessly draping fronds of weed round her legs, retreating then sucking again, the slight drag making her unsteady, thick air seeming to suffocate her. That was when it came - with the swell rising high enough to feel the lift of it at her thighs; you would never forget a thing like that. Something she could hardly call a thought getting into her head, quite tiny and calm at first, mixed deliciously with the breath of the wind in her ears, already starting to spiral through her, huge and terrible. It had always been that way with ideas about painting: once they arrived they could not be contained. Like having someone else's thoughts squeezed into your head. Spreading like some awful disease, until sleep would not come for their fretting; lying in the dark silence, frightened they would never leave her alone. She stood there, buoyed up against the water, filled with something like the fear of flying: something that had coiled her stomach. Filled with an urgent need to be older - ages older. Old enough.

And that had been when it was born; at that precise second, on *Malapet*. That was when she had seen it would be alright. When she had known it might be possible. As if her heart would burst, she had seen how she might work a miracle. Innumerable painted moments superposed, now and not now, fragments of change in space. Paintings she had been frightened to think about. Paintings no one had ever seen before. Her eyes tight closed, her mind filled with the truth of it, at that moment she had been as close to bliss as she would ever be.

A voice, thin and far away, somehow mixed with the flop of the water about her and the streaming of the wind in her ears. Stuart calling her name; she somewhere else, his voice sounding like an echo. Suddenly aware of the glare of the sun, pulling at her hat, realising the others had walked on, little animated dots of white, surprisingly distant, wavering in rising streamers of hot air. All the time the call of Stuart's voice in the sound of the sea.

She must have let Elizabeth tug her back along the shore. Or Stuart? It must have been one of them; she barely remembered. But she would never forget what happened next.

A boy had walked out of the trees and onto the dunes while they had been standing there. Quite tall, older than Stuart, almost grown up. Standing motionless looking down towards them with a slightly defiant look, one hand raised in what could have been a greeting. Staying where he was, waiting for them to come to him. That was the first time she saw Oscar: high on the sand dunes. It was how she would always remember him, the sun blazing round his head. She would never forget that.

Perhaps it was that her heart had been filled with thoughts of painting, but he had seemed strangely woven into it all, part of the bliss. Just looking at him, he had seemed right in a way she had not known before; something sharp and clean about him, hard edges, easy to draw. How she would have liked to draw him. Even his hair seemed right: dark brown, crinkly, almost like a girl's.

He was speaking English. A gentle hesitant voice. Talking about hunting. His name was Oscar Daure, a name the French gave people who covered things with gold. He had seemed proud of that. Talking about the doctor, his uncle - when he wasn't being the Mayor. The faint smile at the little joke seemed just for her. He sounded English. Stuart had blinked at the "Oscar" bit, but recovered and started to stumble out their names, although Oscar knew them already and was sorry nobody had thought to tell them he would be here. He came every autumn with his uncle to shoot the deer and this was a trip to see the lay of the land. He pointed vaguely into the sun and they saw the shimmering form of his little dinghy pulled onto the sand, a line running out to a tree.

Then he was sorry again. He seemed to say sorry a lot: sorry he had disturbed them; sorry if he had startled them. How the English do love to say sorry. To tell the truth, she had barely been listening, looking at the shape of him, missing the pencil in her hand, wanting to draw his head. That was the trouble - she never listened properly when Oscar was talking. It had been ages before she knew what he was saying. That the island was full of deer, not that you saw them often. That they had to be killed to save the herd. Surely that was madness? How she had hated him for saying that.

They never got to the tower. They hardly thought it mattered that day. There was always another; always another year, another holiday. They were wrong, of course: it had been their last. But how could they have known that? All she remembered was sailing round the point to the landing stage, Uncle Albert under his huge white umbrella waiting for them, waving a brush in the air.

He must have been praying she would never learn about those deer and cursing his bad luck. Still, he did his best to keep the peace, indulging her infant protests, hearing her out, even telling her they could always say no – it was their island, after all. Of course, she said no. She'd say the same again, given the chance - not that there ever would be a chance. This Oscar boy, suddenly sheepish, not even looking at her, darting his sly glance at Albert, the two of them sharing a smug smile, thinking she'd not understand. They would do it anyway: shoot the poor things. Asking had just been a game. She too young to know deer exist only to be shot; too young to know the hellish truth of that. The smile had filled her with fury.

What was it Albert said? "You look like you're declaring war on him. At least shake hands with the chap." That had been when she touched Oscar, touched him the first time, him stooping a little to make himself more her height; her thinking that was a good thing to do - something curiously touching in the gesture. So she had relented a little and let him take her hand into his own, trembling slightly. He had been so close she could smell the heat on him. Did he say anything? Perhaps he said sorry again. She could not remember.

She tried to paint the idea after that trip to the island, banging up the stairs to the studio, Mother looking startled, calling out something about supper. It didn't work, of course, even though she worked like a demon possessed. She had tried with thin paint, more or less splashed onto a piece of board that Albert had primed that morning, the primer barely dried. Grabbing it without a thought, desperate to capture the idea before it left her. Wrong on both counts – she was never going quite to capture it, and it would never leave her. Think what you like, obsessions were safe enough with her. Not at all like infections are they?

You don't get cured. Nothing like, drink this and it's gone, apart from the nasty taste. That morning on the beach something had changed and the secret inside her now was a kind of fever. Oscar as well: no cure for him either, crinkly hair and all.

In the end, all she could say of that first painting was "not quite" – which is worse than nothing, of course. She had thrown a big brush onto the table in despair as Uncle Albert came in, watching it bounce onto the floor, daubing a fan of chalky white over the floorboards. She was hardly ever angry, but the frustration had been palpable. There was something there; something queer enough to make even Albert stop and look. He had brought her a cup of hot chocolate and as he leaned down to rescue the brush she saw him dart a glance at her easel. He had stopped asking about her work but had been close to asking then, cocking his head to one side, idly smoothing the bristles of the brush in his stubby fingers, scraping a glob of white onto a rag. He knew what she was up to, right enough. But all he did was tap the bit of board with the brush handle and say, "That was mine, you know". It was the first time she had felt helpless. The first time there was no point asking him - no point asking him ever again. And as she heard him stump off downstairs tears came because he had known that as well.

It was about then she sold her first painting: the one of figures on the Pink House lawn. She'd been in a trance when she'd done it. Juvenile stuff; but confident. Where on earth do you get confidence like that from? Only a madman would have chosen that eyeline – thirty feet up at a tiny window. And no light to speak of, the whole place drenched in soft red, wiping the colour out, killing it. How she'd grinned at that, thinking of Albert and his thing about sunsets. But it came off alright. It helps to be too young to know what's impossible. There was a mood about it, though: her mood. Things like that leak out whether you like it or not and when it works, errors don't matter. It can be as wrong as hell, you just want to go on looking, just want to understand. What happened to it after the little man whisked it away? What became of it? Not that she'd want to see it again. It's a mistake going back.

He'd come all the way from Paris, that chap, bringing the smell of the train with him into the house. It must have been Albert who'd told him to come, but until she worked that out it had seemed a special sort of magic. Like living in a theatre. As if the Angel Gabriel himself had flown in, a little too short for his wings, knowing her secrets. It was the very first thing she sold - he got his money's worth. He spent an hour brooding over the little show in the studio where Albert had hung one of her paintings alongside his own work. She had not signed *The Pink House*, just decorated the bottom of the canvas with an enigmatic image of apple blossom, a shy tribute to Albert's secret love. And the man had offered to buy it on the spot, laughing as she mulishly shook her head. Not altogether how Gabriel should laugh, pretending to take pleasure in a little girl bargaining with him. So he got *Figures on a Lawn*, not quite dry, as compensation. It was the first time she saw that look. It didn't matter that *The Pink House* would never be sold – on account of the apple blossom – the look in those black little currant eyes said it all. It was precocious talent he wanted. It was that brought him to the Pink House to push a bundle of brand-new bank notes into Mother's hands, almost apologetically. When he had gone, Ian spread them out in lines on the kitchen table, making piles of the different pictures on the front. Mother looking on, mumbling, 'He's made a mistake, surely?'

CHAPTER 4

The day before they went home she knew she had to see Oscar again. Stuart had said he had books to take back to the doctor's so she would go with him and Oscar would be there: she had been sure of it. Ever since the abandoned trek on *Malapet* an odd, secret, pervasive pain shaped very like Oscar had located itself below her ribs, assuring her it would only diminish if she could see him. Albert had announced, "You know, I think our Poppy's in love. Who'd have thought it?" She had been too surprised to blush, simply pausing to wonder whether he was right, Mother laying a hand on Elizabeth's arm to stop her saying anything. There had been a little silence, Laura looking solemn. Perhaps she felt she should have been the first. All nonsense, of course. When you are that age, love is just an ache. Even so, the need to see him consumed her. She had cried herself to sleep asking: *what good would seeing him do?* But nothing would have parted her from that secret pain. That mysterious sensation reaching up to her breast, a little like indigestion or a bad cold coming on; something she carried about with her, simply for the

27

oddity of owning it. Stuart changed his mind about the books, quite unconscious of the tragedy he had precipitated: a long-ago girl taking her fever alone into the quiet woods. Just for a walk she had said, deceiving no one. Odd how recollected shame will never fade. Even after all those years she would flush at the thought of that walk past the doctor's house; hopping aside, a car crunching past, somebody waving. That special sort of wave you give a little child by the roadside. Leaving her feeling bereft.

Albert came home with them to London, something he had not done in twenty years, and in the agitated days that followed, and in ways she never properly understood, his being there meant the end of school. There were new uniforms for Stuart and Ian and she had helped sew on Laura's prefect's badge, but all those familiar things were suddenly consigned to another world. It would have been a new school as well and she had looked forward to it. But freshly-cut French bank notes had changed things and in place of school came cheerful Mrs Bickerstaff, arriving each morning, always a little late, to leave her bicycle on its side on the lawn. They would sit at the breakfast table and she would talk about Geography (*Cities of the World*) and History (a feverishly illustrated book entitled *This Island Race*). You could hardly call it teaching with just the two of them, although Mother sometimes came and sat silently on the window seat to listen. Now and then, usually if it was raining, Mrs Bickerstaff would take her aside and they would spend a dispiriting hour, heads bowed over a book on elementary algebra. But since it was never elementary enough for either of them, the futile activity served only to reinforce a feeling that it was all a pretence - reality lay elsewhere.

Exactly where became clear one afternoon not long after Christmas, starting with an old man creaking out of a taxi to stand waiting for her to come down. Paul. She knew him, of course; you could say she had learned what little she knew from his work. In any case, you would hardly forget someone so neat: wide hat, crisp white suit, cotton gloves, ebony cane and brilliant shoes. An oddly theatrical figure in the gloom of a London street. He stood quietly waiting, smoking a thin yellow cigarette, his lined face walnut brown with the sun, impassive. She remembered waving to him from the window – a little girl's excited wave, spotting some exotic bird that had mistaken its proper perch.

They went together in the taxi to the College on Cromwell Road, meeting Albert and a crowd of men waiting on the stone steps. That was when she learned what fame purchased; how celebrity dissolved things at its will and made crooked ways straight. You could see it on their excited faces: how could the greatest artist in France be standing like a human being on the patterned tiles of their floor? They were checking his polished feet to confirm the truth of it. Better say the greatest *living* artist in France, because his fame was so great most of them believed him long dead and that they were witnessing a kind of resurrection. She was ignored, of course; left staring wide-eyed beyond them past the fluted columns and marble staircase, dimly aware of people towering above her, fluttering round the great man. They would surely have walked on without her in a kind of awestruck procession had he not taken her by the hand.

That was all it took. The maker of Great Art took Precocious Talent by the hand and doors opened. She must surely have played some part in it, but all she could remember was life thereafter. A vast white studio lit by skylights: her own space.

She often wondered what the other students made of all this; what they made of her. Most were old enough to be her father. But they soon accommodated to the little girl who could draw like an angel; to the little girl whose effortless paintings seemed to possess some strange power to startle. Above all, they accommodated to the little girl whose work was purchased before it was dry.

A huge man in a fedora hat must have taught her something, but since he rarely spoke, it was hard to see how. He corrected the work of the others at the easel, more often than not scratching at the canvas with his nail, sometimes rubbing a whole day's work out with his fist. But apart from the irritation of his standing behind her, he mostly left her alone. Just once in a whole year he stopped at her side to lean over, close enough to smell his breath and whispered, "You're wasting your time here, my dear." Then, seeing colour start into her face, pointed to her canvas, muttering, "Good ... bloody good."

It must have been about then she began to appear in newspapers: annoying little pieces about the prodigy, although Mother cut them out to keep, nonetheless. Always the same ancient photograph: Poppy aged nine in a print dress. She broadcast on the wireless for something called "Children's Hour", timidly answering questions about what sort of paint she used. Then a second time, by popular request, improbably identifying her hobby as pressing flowers. Once, as she stood waiting for a bus, a complete stranger nudged her companion and both turned to stare.

Towards the end of her third year she must have been about fifteen. Albert had years before fled back to the Pink House and his beloved France. Mrs Bickerstaff, always somewhat intermittent, had ceased altogether, buckling under the unequal struggle, and mornings were now spent at the College. She had sold a dozen or more paintings. Or rather, they had been spirited away by a little man entrusted with this task by Albert. Statements of Account from the bank, faithfully addressed to Mother, itemised giddy sums of money. It seemed strange, but she had become extremely rich.

And Oscar all that time? London is not well made for casual encounters but she knew he was there; having him hard by seemed enough. Often she hurried forward in a crowd to catch up with other broad shoulders, mistaken for his. A couple of times she even jumped down from a bus, only to let some perfect stranger walk by. For a good while - and this was truly rather shameful – looking for Oscar became virtually her only outdoor activity.

It changed one evening. She had decided to walk home, because the smell of the lime trees reminded her of France and she was in no hurry. She came down the steps to find him walking towards her on the other pavement. It was such a startling confirmation of her continual unconscious search that she found herself suddenly immobile, paralysed. Thinking back she was sure her mouth had been open. The wind chose that moment to blow her hair about and she brushed it off. Perhaps he misunderstood the gesture, because he waved and mouthed some sort of greeting. He didn't stop, so you could hardly call it an encounter. But it was to be repeated. There were always days now when she would meet him in the street quite by chance. For surely it was by chance? Either that, or Oscar was keeping her in his sights. It was a bit disappointing to think him bewitched by the stupidity of fame; she had thought more of him. All the same, slipping that chain round his neck was curiously satisfying; certainly enough to be going on with.

She had been frightened to start again on the seascapes, but in the event they came off effortlessly. She seemed to have grown into them. Better than that, she saw how they would end. She understood at last why Albert never worried what next to paint. As she worked to conjure the sea off *Malapet* she knew exactly when it would stop. It would take a fair number to get it all straight, but she had the time. They would come as a piece, at least for her. You could hardly expect somebody to buy the lot, but for her they were a piece. Beyond them, other paintings obscurely stretched out into the years to come, innumerable thousands of them. She would not live to paint them all.

She remembered standing with the little man from the gallery in front of the first, shortly after she had finished it, and explaining he would have to wait until they were all done. He had asked her how many and laughed when she replied lots. He took them eventually. It was her first real show. A tiny gallery in New Bond Street - she remembered nothing of it now apart from Oscar. Because he had been there. She had found herself standing next to a tall chap with a cigarette, thinking how nice he looked and for a few shameful seconds wondering who he was. Until the furious jolting of her heart told her.

'Those deer. I always wanted to ask you. You were going to kill the poor beasts anyway, weren't you? I bet you did.'

It was idiotic. She had blurted out the first thing to come into her head. She blushed to remember it, but he seemed not to notice. It was as if the intervening years had barely interrupted a long conversation and they were back together on *Malapet*. He bowed his head in mock contrition, not denying the deer. It must have been Albert's idea asking him to come to the exhibition. For a second she had found herself wondering whether Oscar had kept a photograph as well. Whether he had cut one out. She bit back asking just in time. Heavens! She had been awkward enough even then. Why would he have kept her photograph?

The gallery was crowded and it was comforting to be conducted by this tall man, no longer a schoolboy. He took her arm at one point to steady her and left it there. It was natural enough: it was what people did, after all. Nonetheless, the soft feel of his hand against her flesh was delicious. Her youth made her the freak in the show, of course. The prize exhibit, more even than the paintings. Inevitably, nobody addressed a word to her. Men moved aside as she approached as if she were sacred, or possibly carried some mildly infectious disease. Younger women sized Oscar up; older women tried out a motherly look on the infant prodigy. A look they had secretly reserved for their own talented offspring. But nobody spoke to her.

How old had she been? At least fifteen. All she could remember was Oscar and an outfit Mother had declared her first grown-up dress. Albert had squeezed her arm and mumbled get your own next time. Not kind really, but the dress really was hideous. The gallery had been mercifully dark. Pools of light picked out paintings against the stark white of the walls. Her paintings: two long walls lost to the sea. You had to admit they took a bit of getting used to although she had been strangely unmoved. After all, once you knew how to do it, it was just another set of tricks. Good tricks, but gone long ago. Although one had come out alright: been at least close to what she intended. She'd stopped painting them after that one. She would never forget how she felt the day she finished it: it was worth living just to feel like that.

The catalogue for the show had arrived in the post a fortnight before, Mother having the usual trouble making sense of the prices. She read them out over the marmalade with a bemused look on her face that made you feel like crying, reading the titles one by one, lips barely moving, wondering out loud whether people really paid that for paintings, because if even some were sold, it would come to an enormous amount of money. Poppy would be richer than all of them put together. She remembered that moment: Mother smoothing the envelope out and quietly putting the catalogue back inside – something to keep. It had been like saying goodbye.

And here was Oscar, answering to the twitch on his chain, standing silently next to her. Oscar the hunter of gold, wondering what he had found. She stood, a glass of water in her hand, feeling too hot, pulling at the back of her dress where it was riding up. How could she have explained to Mother she was indeed rich, whatever that meant? Because the paintings had been sold long before the catalogue had even been printed - all of them. Sold, because that was how things were then. Quite early on a rainy morning, Albert ushering a dozen quiet men into the chill of the empty gallery, canvases on the floor propped up against the walls. She remembered the comfortable lazy talk of old friends gossiping about better days. Men crouching down to stare in silence at her work. She had never met these coldly polite people before; and, indeed, they generally ignored her. But by the end of the morning initials in red ink on a list by the door said her paintings had been sold. That was all it took. "Just avoiding the crush," Albert had mumbled, taking her arm and lighting another little cigar. "Better that way."

That was the end of the sea: the last guttering of a candle before she let it go out. Years she'd spent trying to get that idea out of her head and she wasn't sure, even then, that she had; you can get too close to things, you soon learn that. A dozen or more canvases - all that was left over from God knows how many started. And she would never see them again.

Not quite true - she might see one again. Long before the dealers arrived, while Albert was looking for somewhere to make coffee, a tall man in pinstripe had pushed through the outer door. He shook her hand and prodded Albert in the side of his arm in some kind of shared familiar greeting that made both of them smile. They were grinning like a pair of conspiring schoolboys. For ten intense minutes the man sat quietly on the wooden chair next to Albert, only once leaning over to whisper a secret something that made him nod. Seeing her anxious face, Albert winked. So she might see one picture again, should The Tate decide to show it. The pinstripe paused to initial the list, giving her an enigmatic little bow before springing an umbrella and hurrying off into the rain. A pity, because she would have liked to ask him why he had bought that one – it was the best.

Did Oscar take her to tea afterwards? He must surely have asked – it was the sort of thing he did. Why couldn't she remember? Too much life between, that's why. Or perhaps she said no; she liked saying no to Oscar, liked giving the chain a tweak, just to see. No, she was not that cruel, not then. They must at least have talked a little, Albert in matchmaker mode ostentatiously drifting away. So it may have been tea, but she had no memory of it at all.

The next time she saw Elizabeth, tea had certainly been involved and she had seen Oscar that day. The day of the Great Row, although it had started well enough, as these things do. Elizabeth had come to London to celebrate. "No more school, ever, ever," she'd said, looking enviously at Poppy's frock. "Sorry about the uniform. Mum said I may as well use it up."

They were in a Coffee House in the Strand, bagging a window table like kids, to watch the world go by. Elizabeth had stuffed her green felt hat into her bag and managed to fold her blazer round to hide the badge on the pocket. 'I can't tell you how much I hate this uniform … and you look so nice: so crisp and cool. Still, that's what I'm here for. I've ten pounds, less the fare. Plenty to buy a frock with. I'm going to wear it back home and put these rags in the bag. Never to be worn again. Never to be seen again.'

She hadn't changed. Taller, of course, and lumpy in an odd sort of way, starting to look a little like her mother. She kept asking about Stuart. Where was he hiding himself? Why wasn't he with her? Did Stuart come to London much? He'd come to see her in *Romeo and Juliet*, the school play. She'd been Mercutio and Stuart had laughed out loud because the girl playing Tybalt had been too scared to stab her. She'd heard him in the audience laughing fit to burst. All too embarrassing for words, honest. Anyway, she'd never forgive Mercutio for getting himself done in just when things were getting interesting. She'd gone out with Stuart and Laura afterwards, for dinner; somewhere quite grand and he'd paid. There had been something in her face talking about Stuart, something she was too excited to hide. Something that said Laura didn't get much of a look in that night.

'Gosh … how peculiar.' Elizabeth pointing through the window. 'Isn't that what's-his-name? You know, the mysterious boy. The one on the island. You must remember. Gosh, he's grown.'

Her face on fire, Poppy dared not look. Only three days ago he had walked her home from a concert, turning off to cut across the park. It had been a funny little opera but with music that reminded her of France. He said the piece she liked was called *A Walk to Paradise Garden* and they laughed because, delicious though it sounded, it was really the name of a pub. But the music. Music like nothing she'd ever heard before. Toward the end, there was a passage, just a few notes springing up out of nowhere, lifting your heart with them. And for a second you knew, against all the odds, that the world was alright. It didn't last – who could think that for very long? But you heard them and thought maybe you had a soul in spite of everything. And they stayed with you even then, walking along the narrow gravel path thick with sycamore wings. Perhaps it was the music made them halt, each exquisitely conscious of the other. He was looking into her face as she turned, wondering whether perhaps he would kiss her. He looked as if he wanted to. The music deserved it. After all, the boy and girl on the way to the inn had kissed. She lifted her face a little. It was not a very practised kiss – which was consoling – mostly landing somewhere near her nose. And it was very brief, little more than the lightest touch on her skin. Who would have thought she would feel that for the rest of her life? They walked hand in hand to the park gates; holding hands was alright. Natural enough, all things considered.

And now he was here, today of all days. No accident of course; the chain was not so very long. But it might be days before she saw him next. He would not cross the road now because he had seen Elizabeth. He would think he was in the way, and the idiotic perversity of this conclusion suddenly invaded her. She blazed out, 'Oscar – his name's Oscar.' People looked round, startled.

'I remember now. He was nice. Look, I think he's seen us. Shall I wave back? I remember. Didn't you shout at him that day? Hunting the deer on Uncle's Island – that was it. You shouted at him; you told him off.'

'Of course I didn't shout. And it's not Albert's island. It's ours, remember?'

'I never knew whether Uncle meant all that. Mum said he couldn't really give things away because things aren't like that in France.'

Oscar was still hesitating on the edge of the pavement on the other side of the road. He had an umbrella, although it was sunny that day, not a cloud in the sky. Elizabeth ploughed on. 'And I don't see why you should call him Albert when he's my uncle. It sounds familiar.'

'We work together. I see a lot of him. Whenever he's here ... NO!'

This last as she grabbed at Elizabeth who had jumped up, waving in the window like a schoolgirl. That was what she was - a red-faced schoolgirl in a creased grey skirt a little too long and an unforgiveable blazer with ridiculous green piping. Making faces at the window like an idiot.

Not that it mattered – Oscar had gone.

What was it they had quarrelled about that time? Surely there had been some other row - far worse? Best not think about that. The mood she was in, seeing Oscar take flight, it could have been anything. Poor Elizabeth, expecting little Poppy and finding only a young woman dressed with that peculiarly negligent elegance reserved only for the very rich. Little Poppy trailing a cloud of innocent fame that brought waiters to her table. It must have been hard to take. Perhaps they squabbled about the coffee? Most likely it was Albert she couldn't forgive. All she could recall was Elizabeth, her cheeks ugly with tears, pushing out between the tables only to stumble back, hot-faced and angry, throwing her ten pound note on the table, mumbling, "For the coffee." By the time Poppy was outside, she was too far away, running blindly through the crowd, her school blazer flapping. She never saw her again.

CHAPTER 5

She left for France on her twentieth birthday, telling people she had things to paint that could only be painted in that light. She was in the habit now of going there every summer. It was not as if she intended to stay for ever and if she was to work with Albert there was no choice – he had decided he was too tired to travel. In any case, she was tired herself and the Pink House always worked a kind of magic. She had paintings stored there. As she said, a couple more and there would be enough for an exhibition: she had to earn her keep, after all. It was a sour joke. Everyone said she must be mad. Didn't she know there was a war coming? How could it possibly be safe? Mother blurted out it hardly seemed proper, a young woman on her own, even with the old cook there to keep house. Why didn't she wait to see how things turned out? It seemed that was the only occupation now in England - waiting to see how things turned out, in a kind of stifled paralysis. And since nothing at all ever turned out, she went on with her packing. One thing was sure: for all the fevered talk of war, France was safe enough. In some ways safer than home. Nobody was going to invade France, for heaven's sake! Not with every other man a soldier and every inch of the place defended. No, it was safe enough. You could see what the Germans wanted: mostly settling scores after the last time. You might even say they had a point. But they would hardly try anything with France. How could they?

Hard to imagine herself in that wilful twenty-year old skin, spoiled with reputation. Perhaps she had become not altogether nice. Fame does that to you, grows you another person to live inside; a protection against all the fawning idiots. All the same, no reason for this other self to be so unkind. At times she would see people flinch with hurt and find herself thinking perhaps it's not me doing this. She could easily become not good to know. The worst of it was Oscar put up with almost anything, because of his chain. When work went badly she would tug on it mercilessly, letting him suffer for loving her, knowing he was not one to complain. And he did love her - she was sure of that.

When was it she realised the chain pulled both ways? Some painting must have turned out wrong and the person she lived inside took revenge, telling him to leave her alone, only for his absence to become unendurable. She would ache to see him; to explain that after all they were each part of the same thing. You would hardly say a love affair, more a kind of marriage. Months would pass, for them to take up the thread as if it were yesterday. Months grew to years; painted, comfortable, years. Her going to France was safe enough on the Oscar front, then – no war there either. Oscar would wait, because that was what he always did. One of these days she would do something about that.

It had been Albert's idea to have the exhibition in Saint-Valery. A typical Albert plot. She had been well settled at the Pink House: a final three picture's worth of peace. That morning, he had forgotten to finish breakfast; she remembered that. He'd gone into the little salon to sit hunched next to the wireless set, leaving his coffee on the kitchen table. For days there had been an odd preoccupied look about him. He'd taken to shaving late in the day or sometimes not shaving at all. There was still his painting, of course, but that had become a night-time affair, Albert clattering about in the small hours giving her a reason other than Oscar for sleepless nights.

'You're better up North. You'll not get people here for a show. Not now. They won't make the trip.'

He had come back into the kitchen and was warming his hands on the cup, watery blue eyes looking at her, daring her to ask why. But they had secrets now and she sat silent.

'Anyway, the summer's gone. They come here for the sun, you know that. That's what they come for and they won't get it anymore. Here, what do you think of this?' He was pushing a little red book into her hand, opened out flat. 'You won't know the place, but it's a good gallery and you'll get a decent turnout if they put their mind to it. And they will with your name. It used to be run by a chap I saw a lot of. They won't rip your arms off either, not like that Paris lot. It'll be alright … and like I say, you'll be better off up North.'

The tiny map showed a strip of coast and the deep bite of a river estuary. He pressed a stubby thumb on the page. 'It's on the Somme. Pissarro exhibited there. And Sisley I think, although he never sold much. I did some drawings myself a few years back. They're upstairs. I never made much of them, come to think of it. Mind you, if you're still dead against hunting you'll have to stop your ears. The mudflats there are full of ducks. Flat as pancake the whole place and a tide you'd never believe.'

Ever since she had arrived they had long settled into this conspiracy of mutual deceit, each contriving their own time to crouch over the little orange light of the wireless set, listening to its comforting hum, winding the marker across the printed dial - *Hilversum, Luxembourg, Berlin, Lyon, Paris, Toulouse* – searching for consolation. Not such a bad life if you have a sense of humour – and you had to agree Albert loved his little joke. Because war was everywhere now: all around them. Everywhere but France. So they listened to the crackling voices as the dominoes fell, knowing France, at least, was safe. You would have to be mad to invade France, with the largest army in Europe. Then again, this odd German man did seem a little mad. But France was ready enough. None of that pointless suing for peace in France; just endless maudlin thoughts on the black earth of the Somme, hardly to be trodden on for bones. No, France was safe enough - she was ready. Curious that France should be a woman, with that madman railing about his fatherland. Did that make you feel less safe? Perhaps not, but you bent over the wireless each evening, nonetheless.

She had been born as the last one ended and it was all starting again. She remembered Mother saying we thought we'd stop after Laura. But then, one more, somebody for Laura. You know girls can never play with boys, and I just knew it would be a girl. And there, I was right, wasn't I? As for Ian, we never imagined him at all. These things happen. These things do happen - you'll learn. She had been blushing like a girl when she said that. They really must have thought that was an end to it.

Squinting down at the map of that remote place, listening to Albert shuffle off across the terrace, looking for something: it was quiet, just the two of them in this great rambling place. She'd get him to listen to Mozart tonight. The wind quintet; safe enough, everything held together by the piano. Just the second record, he'd chipped the other one, so now they had to imagine how it all began. But it was enough to know how it ended. She knew Albert would grin at her through the smoke as he tapped out the familiar chords at the end. He wouldn't be coming with her to Saint-Valery. She would have her show there, but he wouldn't be coming. He would tell her tomorrow, or the next day. Or the next week. He would tell her when they were both comfortable with it. After all, it was a sort of end.

Saint-Valery-sur-Somme was a weird place alright – Albert was right about that. Tall houses, incongruous red brick, backed right into cliffs rising straight out of the sand; a straggling breakwater ending at the stump of a lighthouse. Endless boggy tracks meandering through coarse grass with wooden walkways to spare your shoes. As flat as a pancake. Poppy thought of the Devonshire beaches. She'd seen the photographs; the newspapers were full of them now: barbed wire hoisted up on wooden posts, looping between pillboxes. Huge wooden crosses pitched in blasphemous lines. No use here. You'd not stop tanks here. Flat as a pancake as far as you could see – and that was for ever.

It wasn't a chap at all in the gallery, it was an earnest young woman called Hilary something: thin as a rake, beanpole thin. Running everywhere, great strings of amber beads flapping against skinny breasts. Wispy hair, almost blond, crammed under a tiny gesture of a hat. Things had arrived late. Nothing was right anymore; everything was late now; it used to be different. The train was hours late and the van-man refused to wait and she'd had to get another ... no notice at all ... impossible ... but then she'd thought of somebody ... and so on and so on. Fame had inured Poppy to this sort of talk. She had heard it all a dozen times before. She stood inside her unsmiling shell, heard the woman out, knowing better than to say anything; let her chatter peter out.

'Gosh, and here you are. And it's really you. I mean, I feel I already know you. We met at your show in Paris you know. But you'll hardly remember me, it was such a crowd. I was the one asked you about Spencer, do you remember? Anyway, I feel I know you.'

Give this one an inch and she'd take the lot. Poppy summoned a tiny glacial smile, slipping her gloves off. 'They will have sent a plan. The agents. Have you got it? Can I have a look?'

A tormented flap of beads. 'You see, we're a tiny bit squeezed here. But we managed with your plan ... well, close enough ... I think.' Suddenly anxious, she was tugging at the glass door. 'I know you're going to say they're too close, I'm certain you are. And they are ... a tiny bit. But it comes off I think. Honestly.'

It looked fine. For all the flapping arms, the woman knew her stuff. If you discounted the paintings being hopelessly, irredeemably, irrelevant, it all looked fine. Poppy stared blindly at them. Thoughts of war had not touched these images. Not a trace - except perhaps they were a trifle sad. But the sadness had always been there, even when she was just a child. She was famous for it, *dark* being the word that had haunted her since that first show. But you can sell sadness. She could put whatever price she liked, her work sold. For years now she had hated the whole revolting circus. Mother was right: you could set too high a price on things. What did it say, after all? That you could only get worse? She remembered once explaining to Albert - the babble of voices, how nobody really looked at anything. What was the point of painting if people wouldn't look? People just came to be seen and the meaningless frenzy left her feeing numb. He roared with laughter. "God, I was just the same at your age. Take a tip from me - don't get all precious. Numb and rich is a bloody sight better than just numb; I speak from experience. One fine day you'll know it. A fickle lot gallery people, you'll see. Make hay, I say, make hay."

Her hotel smelled of old wood and hot food. The room on the first floor looked across windswept shallows to lines of little boats scurrying back with the tide, men crammed alongside long gun cases. They staggered in pairs across the wet sand sharing the load of sacks, red stains bleeding through the canvas, and found places at the round tables below her window, legs stretched out, drinking pastis, talking quietly of the day's hunt. Looking at the pitiless grey of the open sea.

There was a momentary lull in the restaurant as she came in. Faces turned to look then looked away. The place was filled with the smell of soup, little tureens steaming with fishy garlic and some bitter herb. Better not garlic for the sake of the show. She ordered an omelette and a bottle of Vichy water, the waiter a little too attentive, smirking at his luck serving her. It was ridiculous. Ridiculous and hateful. She felt like shouting, look all you like, I'm just the same as you. Nothing special inside this shell. It's empty. As empty as yours, believe me.

Two men had been standing in the doorway hoping to catch a waiter's eye. The restaurant was full but they inched their way between the tables nonetheless towards one inexplicably empty place. They were in uniform. British, perhaps, but you couldn't be sure now there were uniforms everywhere. Not French, anyway. They didn't look French. The older of the two stood with his hands on the rail of a chair as a waitress hurried over. She was looking awkwardly at the empty desk near the door. One of the two men had his back to her but must have said something because she suddenly reddened.

The young one – he couldn't have been all that much older than Poppy – slumped into a chair, flashing a sigh of relief at the older man. He pulled his cap off, fumbling about looking for somewhere to put it. Eventually he gave up and sat on it, shaking a cigarette out, tapping it idly on the back of the packet, watching the group of men outside, the hunters' quiet voices floating through the open window. One reached down into a canvas bag at his feet. There was the flash of bright feathers, blue and black, a thin neck flopping across his wrist. He handed the bird to a waiter through the open window and the two of them spoke together for a moment, looking out across the grey rush of the incoming tide.

As if he felt her eyes on him, the younger man turned abruptly, catching her unawares. He gave a mock frown then raised a glass in an odd ironic gesture, as if he knew her. She flushed and turned away, cursing again the devilish asymmetry of fame. Now that half the world seemed to know her she felt perpetually naked. It was only when she turned back, resolved to stare him down, that he half rose from the table and she recognised him. God, it was too late. There was a look of hurt in his face she had never seen before. It was the uniform, all that stiff cloth doing what it was meant to, driving the life out of him. Then again, there had been only his face to go by and she had dared not look at his face. But something in her had seen his hair - crinkly, almost like a girl's. Something was causing that pounding in her breast. She'd thought about that hair often enough. He had seen the look on her face, the one she reserved for the importunate who believed they knew her. And the funny hurt look, like a little boy, turned her heart over.

It was getting late. The card for the show said nine, but nobody kept to that. There would be nobody there yet. She sat on, her head bowed, thinking she really would have to go soon, but making no move. The two men ate in companionable silence. She glanced down to find her plate had gone. A china coffee pot on a tiny silver tray had taken its place. She must have eaten the omelette. She couldn't remember: perhaps they'd just taken it away. Had she ordered coffee? She couldn't remember either. It was already late, although they expected her to be late. This was France after all; everybody would be late.

She played with the coffee cup, trying so hard not to look it became ludicrous. Finally, the scrape of a chair and she risked a glance. The older man was standing. Now she could see him, he seemed altogether too old for a soldier of any kind, deep lines cut into his face. He had a tiny clip of a grey moustache. Long leathery hands mottled with liver spots. He swung round abruptly and gave her a brief nod, almost as if she were one of the party, reaching down for his cap.

'I'll be off. Got to see a man about a dog. Food was fine, but I knew they'd be slow.' He took a little while to get into his stride, stiff from sitting down. 'I'll walk. Transport's outside: don't break it – it's not mine.' And with a faint smile at the feeble joke and another nod to Poppy he was gone.

She let the waiter fuss around her table, waiting for her to stand. She was dreadfully late; she really should go. She let him carry her chair across to the other table, leaving it at an angle so she would be not quite a guest. She sat down, putting her pointless little silver bag on the cloth and held out a hand.

'Forgive me. I'm awful at faces. Lots of painters are. And you being here, of course. The last place I thought you could be. So you see, you'll have to forgive me. And I only have a minute: I'm late for something.'

'No, I had the advantage of you. I knew you were here. After all, your name is all over the place.' He laughed at her look of puzzlement. 'The posters: you must have seen them. Not too hard to track you down. We call it reconnoitring in my trade. And I wasn't going to miss your show.'

How odd they should meet here of all places. But if not now, then sometime; and if not here, then somewhere. That was how it always happened. They were a pair when it came to it. It really did seem inevitable.

He was talking about how she piped up and said no. It must have been being in France that reminded him of the girl who had a thing about hunters. Teasing her about this hotel - packed full of them. Poppy found herself laughing as well. Laughing with him, buoyed up that he remembered. Asking about the deer, all the while thinking about her first night at Albert's house years ago. A little girl at the dinner table on the terrace of the Pink House, peeping up at the spangle of candles through old glass, too rapt to speak. Moths flying to the scent of flowers blown from the night garden, musk and cloves. Gillyflowers, Albert called them. Everything filled with itself – everything first, separate, strange, kind and wonderful.

It was like that now: Her show forgotten, she was a little girl again, large-eyed and silent, listening to his voice, a million secret pleasures settling on her skin. She barely heard the faint rustle of turning waves at the breakwater, sea air through the dark of the windows bending the candle flames, making them flutter. All the time he was talking, laughing, joking, brushing hair back out of his eyes, resting his hand a second on hers as she stopped him filling her coffee cup.

She must have said something. Surely she spoke? He was asking questions, so she must have replied. But she only remembered hearing his voice as the peaceful bustle of the room retreated. Tiny glasses appeared brim full, each with a meniscus of Armagnac. And they were quite alone. The waiter at the desk sat looking at the evening paper folded over. It was dreadfully, hopelessly, late.

He was talking about somebody's wife. He must have been for a while so she ran to catch his words. Talking about a wife. Talking about his marriage. He was marrying somebody; was married already. Something like that. Somebody called Emily - a stupid sort of name. It was a mistake. How could he have married anybody? He was too young for one thing, just a boy. They were both too young. They were just children waiting to grow up. And it was impossible because Oscar was hers. He always had been.

No you can't be. No you can't be. The person that lived inside her was screaming now. Screaming inside her head. How could he not hear that? He saw her frozen smile and went on talking, perhaps a little awkwardly, fidgeting with the coffee spoons, lining them into rows. The murmur of his voice saying Emily was at home, wherever that was. So they had a home, did they? Emily would have loved to be here, loved to meet the Poppy she'd heard so much about. *No she wouldn't. I'd damn well see to that.*

She managed to stand, casting around for her bag. He took her arm as they reached the door. It wasn't far to walk.

People had spilled into the warm dark outside the gallery, filling the street with the scent of cigarettes and wine: an impromptu party gathered on the pavement round some bright spark who had collared a couple of bottles and a tray of things to eat. The crowd fell silent for a second as she arrived then made up for it by talking all at once. Through the open door there was Hilary, heroically smiling, a little anxious. The amber beads came flying out to meet her in waves of pent up energy. She pulled Poppy inside the doorway until she winced with the force of it.

'Did you get lost? We were wondering. Almost time for search parties.' Eying the tall figure standing outside, whispering, 'Is he with you? I forgive you. Where did you get him?' She was trying not to sound arch, giggling, twisting round, scanning the table for a clean glass. 'We'd better get him a drink. Don't worry, I'll see to it. Stay there.' Another grab at the arm.

'Seriously darling, don't move an inch. You're just perfect where you are.'

She darted away to the back of the room, suddenly stopping to spin round, pointing to the walls, arms stretched out wide. She looked a little drunk.

White cards had been pinned to the wall alongside the paintings, each with its own red spot. All of them. Hillary's eyes were alight with the glory of it. An empty feeling consumed Poppy. It was always that way. She wouldn't see them again. All those hours and she'd not see them again. Like Oscar. She'd not see him again either.

She watched him easing his way quietly along the walls, stopping now and then to look, and wondered what his Emily would think. What would this inane Emily think of Poppy's soul? Would she like it? She was sure not. She hoped not. People stepped back as the unfamiliar uniform made a narrow opening through the crowd, down one wall and back. Until again he was standing at her side.

'Can you get outside a minute? I have to go. There's something I want to say. Something I have to tell you. Just a second, before your friend comes back.'

'She's gone to get you a drink. And she's no friend of mine. I hardly know her.' But she let him lead her out into the soft salty air to hear the something, whatever it was. *I made Emily up – she's just a joke.* No it wouldn't be that, would it? Of course, it wouldn't. It was in that moment she realised she knew nothing at all about him. How could she explain she had lived with him all these years and barely knew him. You couldn't explain that. Not to Emily.

The sea was everywhere, invisible beyond the low wall, slightly menacing. A warm dampness hung about the place, invading your clothes. Where the sea began was complete darkness. The chatter of innumerable birds came to them across the flat marshes. She had a fleeting image of floating chilly nests and felt as if her heart would break.

Thoughts of Oscar had somehow worn her out. How could she explain that? She glanced at his face, suddenly taut with something and was sure he knew. As sure as she could be of anything: he knew. In the restaurant it had shone in his eyes. He loved her. And he had something to tell her. But it wasn't going to be that – not that at all.

'Look'.

They were alone in the silence and she recoiled at his whisper.

He checked himself. 'I could be shot for saying this.'

She smiled into the dark and he sensed it, suddenly falling into a whisper that stopped her heart.

'That man: you met him earlier ... well, you saw him. He'd have me shot without a second thought in his head. No, I'm serious.'

He was close now, his voice a low rumble in her ear. 'You should get out of here. You're going back to England after this?' He barely waited for her invisible nod. 'Right. Soon as you can.'

He straightened up and held out a hand. Poppy took it. It was as if they had never touched before. Perhaps for the last time they were children again on *Malapet*, making peace. She waited until he relaxed his grip and moved away to the side of the little black car. He opened the door and climbed inside.

'I might see you in London then. I know how to find you. You're hard to miss, you know. You'll remember what I said.'

After he had gone she stood for a long time looking into nothingness, letting sea mist ruin her hair. Far away to her right a flash of white stone reared out of the dark as the breakwater caught the lights of his car. Then he was gone.

CHAPTER 6

She returned to London feeling she had given birth: there was now Emily to reckon with. Someone she hardly believed in. She had never expected to share her Oscar, he had always seemed a peculiarly personal possession. Yet he had gone. What's worse, gone of his own accord, leaving nothing but space. It served her right for thinking space was her domain; for thinking artists had that all worked out, because she found herself terrified to look into nothingness. She imagined it was what grief felt like: something dull and permanent, not quite a pain, that had decided to live with her through the days of gas masks and sandbags. After all, separation defined the normal for everybody now. Suddenly, there were soldiers everywhere. London was a city asleep on a cliff and the fact nothing seemed to hold together became a kind of promise. The sense of bleak dislocation everywhere was oddly consoling. Perhaps Emily would not hold either.

She rented a flat and a studio in Battersea. It was the best the agents could find, they said, now that the army seemed to be taking everything. And if it wasn't the Army it was the Air Force, you couldn't get decent studio space for love or money. She did not tell them that she had only one of those available. The studio was a queer sort of place, mostly tiled in white, but it suited well enough because it was very large and for what she had in mind she needed room. It had been the surgery of a German dentist, now hurriedly returned to his native Hamburg. Part of an undistinguished red brick terrace in a back street, living out its last days. Not that anyone yet knew those were its last days. Remains of the missing dentist lay where he had left them and for some reason the wreckage of this man's abruptly abandoned life set her on fire. Ten hours a day she worked, barely stopping to eat, squeezing the mystery out of that sense of dislocation, making a painting huge enough to put an end to herself. The whole conception was futile. She had never painted anything so big and was continually forced too close, standing on steps to peer at it, wondering whether the thing worked. It seemed that the doing of it was all that mattered. What else was she expected to do? What else, with that woman for ever peering over her shoulder?

Each day if there was sun, bars of shadow fell across the work and made her stop. It was never for long. That morning, as she stepped back, a shape caught her, held her in mid-step, tottering like a child when the music stopped. There was a running contour of yellow pink, flushed more red now with the sun, showing the cusp of a neck running down to the breast. The aureole of a nipple. Naked then, this unwonted accident. And enough of a face – certainly the turned edge of a nose – under a cascade of hair. Quite a pretty head, but turned away: no eyes. God, she was losing her mind. Albert once did something like this, but he had meant it, planned it, practised it for days: a figure dressed in pink and blue buried against apple blossom. All so cunningly made into one piece you doubted anyone could be there. He'd intended that miraculous thing – it was his goodbye to somebody he had loved. But this had simply emerged to stop her heart. Since they had never met – not been introduced - you could understand this Emily looking away. Hard to get the tip of a head like that with so little of a line. You could try for months to get that. What was the word? "Haughty" – that would do quite well.

What became of that painting? Not that it mattered; you would not want to look again at all that pain. Certainly would not want to see those shameful alterations. The thing had surely gone with the rest of the street, consumed in the fire of a minor act of war, along with the file cards, the dental wax and the dreadful pump-up chair. As she finished it, teetering inexpertly on an improvised ladder, that spiteful portrait by Otto Dix came to her: *Dr Koch in his Surgery*. Where had she seen it? Germany, surely. Only Germans painted things like that. But she knew well enough why the thought had come. Hadn't the artist cuckolded the good doctor even as he painted him? What did that say? What had Oscar done? What was he doing now? Misery leaked onto the canvas like a stain. Why the hell should she care what became of it?

Towards the end, the mood in London changed. No one waited anymore to see how things turned out, not even Mother. It was plain how things would turn out: England would be invaded. Bombed first, then invaded. When German soldiers tired of Belgium they would be finding new beds in London. What would they do, these invaders? What might they do? Any woman would wonder that. And she could not even speak German. In panic she had telephoned Oscar's number, shamefully holding the receiver at arm's length, watching the pulse in her wrist rise, waiting for the unbearable sound of his voice. But it rang out with no reply.

They said airfields were being built along the East coast. She took to spending time at Liverpool Street station, sitting in the Waiting Room with a pot of tea, watching men in blue uniforms come and go. Most days now, foreign children, dozens of them, would spill out from trains to stand in bewildered groups on the platform, whispering together in languages she could only guess at. But never Oscar. She watched little Polish girls, holding hands two by two, unnaturally polite, waiting patiently to be counted by harassed women with lists. German boys in short trousers, tiny knapsacks strapped to their backs, large-eyed and silent. It was baffling: why send their children here? Alone, what's more, with little more than a suitcase. Hardly out of harm's way - you couldn't say that. When you might be bombing your own children, faith in the charity of your enemy seemed insane. Perhaps he really was mad; he sounded mad. They looked scared, these lost infants, with their strange clothes. Sometimes the men in blue would call across, trying out words in German, hoping for a smile perhaps. They were little more than boys themselves.

One evening she had been scurrying down Charing Cross Road, her head bowed against a sudden shower, hoping for a taxi. No umbrella, because it should not have been raining. In France, days that start as fresh and blue never end in rain. The pavement was blocked with people spilling out from the shelter of a vast doorway. As she tried to push past, an old woman took her arm, smiling in a sick sort of way, pulling at her. 'You're coming in are you? We're best out of all this. It's not started yet. There's still time.' She didn't sound mad at all.

Inside, the sour smell of damp wool and dead candles, cold and very dark, iron shutters bolted against the stained glass, blocking the light. She often thought of God, even prayed now and then when Emily had been a particular torment. But God had surely stopped going to church. Why would He come in here? He surely had more sense? There were chairs, but no one was sitting. High above the little knot of people, barely visible in a carved pulpit, a reedy little asthmatic voice intoned, stopping now and then to cough:

'We pray for deliverance, O Lord ...'

The woman at her side mumbling with the settled intensity of the insane, holding a prayer book unopened in awkward arthritic hands, squeezing it in concert with the piping sing-song words, her whole body shaking. Why were they in this place? The woman's fear was like a contagion. *Deliverance*? Deliverance from what? The piping voice stopped, only to began again louder, the psalm horribly familiar:

O Lord, thou hast searched me, and known me.

She was a schoolgirl again, long before the days of Mrs Bickerstaff, a little girl, knees chafing on the coarse cover of the hassock, head resting on the wood of the pew in front, something like rage boiling inside her. How dare her heart be searched? Who dared say she could not escape this person who searched her and knew her; knew her every secret thought? There were secrets she wished to keep. Who was this person you could never get away from, not ever, however hard you tried? Who had such horrible ideas?

She was already stumbling outside into the rain, desperate not to hear. Too late, words chased her, faint but clear enough: *if I make my bed in hell, behold, thou art there.* No, she had not wanted to hear that. Not today.

God was fond of His little joke: as she stood shaking with fury, a taxi drew alongside. She clambered in, overwhelmed with thoughts of war, the certainty of it flooding through her like a fever breaking, like a kind of relief. She craned forward to see, but the newspaper boy had thrown a sack over his box against the rain. On the corner by the underground station there was another: nothing but the name of a horse and a starting price, the chalked scrawl blurred with rain.

Nothing on the wireless either. Certainly nothing about war. A sugary crooner singing, 'Darling *je vous aime beaucoup*,' the French accent execrable. Perhaps it was meant that way. She listened on in spite of herself, thinking of Albert far away, sitting on the terrace after dinner, smoking one of his little cigars. He would be painting into the night, he did that now; perhaps the colours a little uncontrolled - you could blame the light for that - but they were things you would want to look at, all the same.

'Je ne sais pas what to do; Vous avez completely stolen my heart.' Except he hadn't: he had no call to steal, he must have known that. He had been given it years ago. A gift. Before he knew he wanted it. And there was the nub of it - perhaps he never knew. He had not stolen her heart, completely or otherwise: he had done his stealing elsewhere and there were three of them now. And three's a crowd, anybody knows that. The damned song was right about one thing - she didn't know what to do.

Oscar had told her to go back home and she'd done as she was told. Obeyed like a good girl; back to dislocated England. And it had been a monstrous mistake. England was not her home now, it was his: his and his Emily's. If you tried to paint in England, misery leaked in with the damp. Even the sunlight here seemed worn out. Oscar had told her to get away from the mudflats of Saint-Valery - away from the bright feathers and bleeding corpses - and she'd done as she was told like a good little girl. England was a poor exchange, fearful and falsely hearty; Oscar and his Emily, holding their breath, waiting for their war. The thought broke your heart. This was a bad place to be, right enough.

Travel was easy if you were going the wrong way. The morning she stood on the platform at Victoria, thinking only of the South, the trains were empty. She had to change in Paris, of course, but there was no hurry about that. That walk through the heat of the evening, past the smell of restaurants opening, was like coming home. There was something comforting hearing your footsteps click down streets quiet after the rush of the day, a dreamy calm everywhere, bits of broken music floating down from open windows. Old women sitting on doorsteps leaning back, getting a breath of air, looking up to nod a greeting, maybe even a smile. Nobody would be waiting to see how things turned out in France: things would look after themselves.

The night train at the Gare d'Austerlitz was always late to leave, but it hardly mattered. If you pushed the stiff blind to one side there were porters, idle at last, lighting cigarettes, leaning on their trolleys. You had only to wait and the whole silent pattern would slide away. She loved the night train. Loved to sit up in bed and let her head fall forward, knowing she was asleep, knowing she would wake to sombre lines of trees and a foreign sky. After fitful sleep under a single stiff white sheet, a little cold in the night, you would wake to see dawn flying blue and gold over a landscape infinitely wider than the hedge-bound fields of England. Endless to the far horizon. She would sit on the edge of her bed, hearing approaching taps on cabin doors, murmured voices, the smell of coffee. And she would be going home.

When the waiter let the blinds up, a blinding French sun would catch the glass vase, sprinkling light round the cabin. There would be a tray with white china, coffee, croissants, little bowls of jam, too many spoons, the starched cloth folded. It was always like this. There was no war here. France never changed. And still South, past parched fields, men easing their backs to watch the train. South, until afternoon spread out under a dangerous blue sky. She remembered Oscar then, dressed in his blue, and was irritated that a little of the war had come with her. It was an odd blue - when she had first seen that colour she had wondered what war would be like for blue men. What became of them when they fell to ground? It was an impossible thought.

'I thought you'd be back – you never do what you're told.'

Albert was sitting on the terrace, a single place for dinner set on the table. She had taken him by surprise, walking round the house and across the lawn, dumping her case at his feet. He made to get up then sank back, laying a book face down on the table. He looked smaller, his face a little pinched, a kind of grey weariness that his grin could not disguise. 'I said to Pia, she'll be back, you see.' He looked genuinely pleased. 'You do realise it's not a good idea? Still, you're welcome, you know that. I'll get her to lay you a place. You must be tired'

'You're the tired one. You look all in. What's up?'

'Things to do, you know. Things to do. Now the light's started to draw in, you don't get so much time. I'm still better with the light, remember?'

'And I'm not, I suppose?' She smiled to acknowledge the old joke, then took his hands, brushing a kiss against his face. He had not shaved that day.

He looked up, wide-eyed, a malicious smile on his face. 'How did it go, then? Saint-Valery? You never said. It was a good while back but you never said. I thought you'd write but you never do.'

'You were right. It was a nice little place. A reasonable crowd. Sold well.'

'Not that the artist saw much of it, by all accounts. You see, some people do bother to write.'

'You mean by Oscar's account. It was him wasn't it?' She felt obscurely pleased. 'Like a gossipy old woman, you are.' She waited for him to say something but he remained looking lazily into her eyes. She gave in, looking down, cursing herself. 'You want me to tell you I met him there. And you know that perfectly well.'

'He's a nice chap. Are you smitten?'

She found herself flushing with annoyance. 'Don't be silly. I barely know him. And he's married - pretty well - you didn't know that.'

'I did as a matter of fact. You'd be surprised what I know. It's gossiping that does it. Funny affair from what I gather. I remember that day you fronted up to him on the island, though. No bloody hunting here you said, or words to that effect. I wish I could have got the two of you then, but I didn't have a pencil with me. My God, but you looked something – like a baby avenging angel. Then again, you've always been a bit queer.'

She straightened her skirt and looked down at her hands. 'Queer or not, I'm in need of a wash. Now if there was hot water, a bath would be nice. I don't suppose?'

'You don't suppose right. Send a telegram next time. There's no hurry. I'll get Pia to move us inside; it'll be getting damp.'

When she came down to the dining room Albert wasn't there and a half-finished glass of whisky on the table somehow set her heart racing. His chair had been pushed back. From the little salon next door, a muffled sound of excited voices from the wireless piled on top of each other, none making sense.

Suddenly he was standing half in the doorway, still listening, looking back into the room behind him. The little cigar in his hand had smoked itself out.

'No, you shouldn't have come back. But too late now.'

Poppy went over and took his hand, drawing him into the room. Letting him sit on the edge of a chair, eyes darting nervously round. She tried to laugh. 'What's this too late about then? Turning me out, are you?'

'It's serious. They say German troops might move against Poland. We'll be in a war over this, you see.'

It sounded quite orderly, "Move against." Something considerably less than violent. And who was "we"? She found herself feeling irrationally angry. She wanted to say, it's nothing to do with me, I'm not in a war, I'm here because I want no part in this. I refuse. She remembered Oscar's face all those years ago when she had told him about the deer and there had seemed too little air in the world for both of them. She was conscious of the same massive silence inside her head, as if she were drowning. A moment's dizziness muffled the words from the wireless set in the other room, as if from under the sea. The talking had stopped at last. There was music. Somebody was singing *Je ne sais pas what to do*; an execrable English accent. Muted dance music, the tempo very strict, spoiled by the leaves outside scuttering over the stones of the terrace.

Pia bustled into the room and stood looking at the two of them, red-eyed and indignant.

Albert got up. 'Yes, I suppose we'd better eat something. It'll be getting cold.'

CHAPTER 7

Of course, Oscar had been right, she should have kept to her word, done as she was told, stayed in England like a good girl. Idiotically, if there is to be a war, home always seems the best place to have it. This time she had done something really mad: the whole world about to catch fire and she runs into the woods to hide like a schoolgirl. And why? Because a man she barely knew loved somebody else. Crossed in love, that's what it came to and she couldn't quite let him go, hanging on to his coat-tails like a child: Oscar, far away, cherishing his Emily, planning for his war. You could only blush for the shame of it.

So the Pink House it was to be. Paradise, if you didn't think too hard about certain things. An ancient Pia Berri – who let the holiday children call her Cook - quietly making everything work. And hidden behind her ample skirts an unseen army of others: boys fetching groceries, men carting ladders about, women washing, women cleaning, woodcutters cutting, gardeners gardening. Whole armies of gardeners, come to think of it;

altogether the wrong sort of army now. How could she live here, miles from anywhere, when war started in earnest? It was madness. Albert painted all day (all night too if he felt like it), and she was set fair to be the same. When she was really on fire she quite simply did nothing else, hardly noticing how meals appeared. What if all this ended in war, as surely it must? England suddenly seemed unbelievably remote. She had made a mistake, no two ways about it.

Although in the days that followed you could not say anything much changed. There was anxiety, of course, but that is less than fear and you can learn to live with it. You walk in the garden and the light is just that trifle odd, sharper than itself. You look around and there is nothing new to see, if only your heart would stop galloping. Apart from the wireless, no way of knowing anything at all, as Poppy passed her vacant moments walking on the Pink House lawns, stepping round memories.

The two of them fell into a new pattern of days as it gradually became clear that Holland, then Belgium, had embraced their own new reality. Wireless voices became more emphatic. It was clear enough that *something* was happening, but far away, and the summer seemed not to care enough. As if to secure the point, a *canicule* set in, heat filling the air with the throb of cicadas and the scent of burning resin. The talk at the village shop was of German bombs and refugees. The newspaper showed grainy images of cars abandoned at the roadside. Filled with Belgians, it said: rich Belgians packed in motor cars. But no Belgians came to the Pink House, rich or otherwise, and summer made the inexplicable plight of Belgians unreal. As for bombs, why would bombs fall here?

In the heat there was no choice but to work with windows open wide. Even so, paint dried on the brush and she was put to using too much turpentine. Long yellow-bodied hornets, drawn to the scent, lazily exploring the studio, nosing silently between stacked canvases. Through those endless dog days, an unfocused anxiety, no more than a vague tight feeling about the head, unsettled her. She began avoiding supper talk with its scraps of trivial rumour and settled for uncertainty. It was enough that *something* was going to happen: the hammer would eventually fall.

To her surprise, work went well. Albert helped stretch canvas over two huge frames, holding tacks in his mouth and beating inexpertly with a hammer driving wedges in.

'God, you'll need a ladder for these. I've got something that will do the job. Old library steps. But you'll regret it, my girl. Nobody will buy big things anymore. They want something you can put under your arm. Think of the transport. I ask you - who's going to do the carriage?'

He regretted saying it immediately. There were things now it was best not to say; events it was best not to anticipate. The future had become forbidden territory – you didn't venture there - so Poppy just smiled. After all, he knew well enough why she was doing it. Finishing something this big would take forever. Wars didn't last forever; she knew that much.

Although it was only a walk away, they avoided the doctor's house. He was Oscar's uncle and that was reason enough. But he was also the Mayor. The Commune was tiny, but he would know more than they wished to hear. If there were hideous events – and it seemed possible now - he would know of them. It was a cowards' solution, born of a conviction that what they did not know could not harm them. This new estrangement endured for weeks until, eventually, it was J-P himself who visited. Albert had always called him that, even when they were children. She could only guess what it meant: Jean-Paul? Jean-Pierre? Too late even to guess. Then, he had simply been someone Stuart visited for hours on end, nursing his resolve to become a doctor as soon as he grew up.

J-P arrived late one afternoon, a familiar slender figure with his white hat, pushing through the gap at the edge of the woods and jumping down onto the lawn. Her heart began its habitual pulse, of course; she could do nothing about that. But he was quite alone. Oscar would not be visiting here again, not till the war's end, perhaps not ever, given the blue uniform. Perhaps not ever, given Emily. Her resolution had been not to think about Oscar, but she sat with the two of them, catching the last of the heat, hoping to hear his name. Sipping pastis, hearing the doctor's news. That is how aniseed became the taste of defeat. Not that she was sure defeat came into it; he was mercifully vague. He talked of armistice. For days the wireless had filled the place with that word. France, through some inexplicable lapse of will, had secured the fruits of defeat. By some sleight of hand she would not be the next domino to fall. The three of them sat staring into the huge ball of the setting sun, thinking of war averted. Sitting silent until long shadows reached across the grass and the air fell suddenly damp. Twice Pia came to the kitchen door, gesturing that dinner was ready, but they sat on, listening as the doctor began again, explaining what it meant to yield with honour. Whatever else, it was no sort of defeat; anyone could see that. He leaned forward to explain to her in particular that an army could be a shield as well as a sword. She could only think what odd creatures men were. What nonsense, when all that mattered in the world was that Oscar survived it; that somehow, by some miracle, he came out alive – unscathed.

J-P would not stay to eat, but before he left he took a letter from his pocket and spread it out on the table for them to see. It was addressed to him as Mayor, although the author was unclear, the signature buried in a cascade of hastily overprinted titles and offices. Someone had stamped a tiny red swastika symbol in the corner, not quite straight: it was the first she saw. Albert mumbled rapidly through it. Written in old-fashioned elevated prose of a kind that had almost disappeared, it sounded like a sermon or an end-of-term speech. It was hard not to smile. About a new order and a new government, neither French nor German, collaborating against a common enemy, the quixotic stubborn English. Anyone could see this was no sort of defeat. As Albert finished, the doctor took back the top page and staring sightlessly at the scrap of paper told them Paris had fallen. Did they know Paris had fallen? Not moved against - this time the word was fallen. It sounded somehow worse. Albert glanced at her and went back to read the bit about the common enemy.

The next day a dusty car brought a man down the bumpy drive. J-P had said it would happen, nonetheless she spent a sleepless night imagining her first encounter with a German soldier. She knew virtually no German. But this man was alone and not even properly German, speaking with the odd nasal accent you got in the North – Alsace perhaps. Unhappy in the heat, sweaty in thick clothes, his shoes covered with the red dust of the forest tracks.

He declined a drink and shook his head as Albert gestured him inside, standing on the bottom step of the stone staircase breathing heavily as if the heat was too much, craning his neck, trying to count the windows. He peeled a single page from a sheaf of papers and handed it to Albert, asking him to fill it in without delay, gave a nod to Poppy and was gone. Albert was left with his hand still outstretched in greeting. As they walked back round to the terrace he stopped to glance at the paper.

'They want a list of who lives here … and how long … and nationality. That last's a bit of a facer, you know. All things considered best not to be English I should think. Not at the moment. None too popular, the common enemy.' He blew a circle of smoke into the morning air and grinned at Poppy. 'I'm French – I bet you didn't know that. I think you'd better be as well. J-P can fix that for you – it's what Mayors do. Your passport's no good, though. Did you bring it? I always forget mine. Come to think of it …'

He broke off and lumbered back into the house. She heard the door to the library squeak open and heavy footsteps echo across the bare boards. His face appeared at the window waving a piece of folded paper, fumbling with the handle, yanking it open with a squeak and leaning out.

'This'll do … Have to change the date though.'

When he came back outside he was grinning like a schoolboy.

'She got this on a trip to Austria, to get across the border. It looks official enough … really grand … photograph and all.

There's just the date or you'll end up too old. I always think a little forgery before breakfast gets the day off right, what d'you think?'

He had passed her a sheet of yellowing card, perforated as if it had been torn out of a book. There was a photograph of a young woman crudely glued in one corner, too much contrast making the eyes no more than ovals of black. Poppy looked at him. 'Who is she? It could be anybody.'

'I knew her a long time ago. But she could be you, my girl, that's the point. Don't worry about the date, although I doubt old dusty shoes will bother to look. A drop of summer rain is going to fall on that date this very afternoon, just you see.' He was still laughing as he turned back to the form lying on the table. 'List all occupants present who are members of the Jewish race. Sounds mad. We're the only occupants, we two and Pia. I'll put "none" and leave it at that.'

'Why do they want to know, anyway? Is it something to do with the church? What about Paul? He's Jewish. He's the only one we know. He's here often enough.'

'He's not an occupant. I know, I'll put "none known," will that do?'

Poppy did not reply. She was poring over the tiny photograph. A defiant face stared at her, hair pulled back from a high forehead, the hint of a smile indulging whoever was operating the camera. There was a name irregularly typed across a dotted line: "Lucile Beyrou," a hasty signature at the bottom in blurred rusty ink.

Nobody asked to see the paper, least of all the shabby man in the little car. But J-P had been right about one thing: England's war was lost. The wireless was quite clear about that. It had been over before it had had time to begin. Much the same as France, in fact. Things had moved against England because there was nothing left but the channel. The talk was now how the New France had assisted the moving against – the phrase was vague enough, after all. Each evening the wireless confirmed yet again that England had fallen. Poppy saw tanks and men lumbering across the windswept beaches of Devon, her heart filled with a numb terror. England had yielded with honour and she had not been there to see it. She had become someone else: Lucile Beyrou was trapped.

As summer slowly spent itself, the war England had lost - inexplicably already lost – settled to solemn speeches on the wireless. Only as things started to disappear did anything at all seem real. The end of coffee was the first call on Lucile Beyrou, as her name was painfully transcribed by the grocer into an improvised ration book and *coffee* marked with a cross. The ration was not enough and soon there was no point to the cross – there was no more coffee. Because Pia was too old to walk, Lucy trudged every day now from the Pink House to the village through an enchanted landscape, thinking only of the empty tin in the kitchen.

Bread was next. There was a morning where breakfast found Pia weeping in the kitchen because there would be no more bread. For years a succession of little boys on bicycles brought bread to the house. All the boy had brought that morning was news the baker had closed and moved back to live with his mother. Perhaps somebody else could try, but you can't make bread without flour. As autumn quietly sloped into winter, Lucy learned that war was squabbling queues at the grocers; war was the butcher closing early, then closing altogether; war was shamefully stealing a head of maize from an abandoned field. Above all, war was feeling hungry.

The wireless changed: less about England now. Talk of England left the exact nature of the defeat vaguely unresolved. New voices harped on now, day after day, about Jewishness; you could hardly avoid it. Agreed, this yielding with honour had been no kind of defeat, would an earlier France have yielded? That was the question. What was it you murmured at the memorial stones each November, wrapped up warm against the chill? As names were called, one by one, you muttered, *mort pour la France*. It seemed worth saying, eased the pain, knowing they wouldn't come home. Things had changed, the wireless was sure of it. A kind of weakness had wormed its way in. People didn't think in the old way anymore, and why was that? Who was telling the lies? After all, if you were a Jew you didn't have a country to die for. All you had was a weird sort of religion. They were bound to think differently, the Jews, even the French ones. Although they weren't what you could call really French because they wouldn't let you forget about their Jewishness. You could almost say they were pretending to be French. Rich as well: most of them were rich; pretty well all rich. You had to ask how they managed that. Were all these rich people spending their days looking for bread? The wireless had to ask the question, it was only reasonable, there was a certain logic to it.

When the man came back eventually, he was in a different car. Two bored Gendarmes slumped in the back had wound the window down so that they could smoke. The man refused to come in, standing in the doorway, peering inside, holding out the paper, asking what "none known" meant. Albert took it from him. 'I should have said none. The answer's none.'

It was well into winter when Paul moved in. On the steps of the College that day in London he had seemed a kind of god. He arrived late one afternoon, a tiny figure in a cheap raincoat with an umbrella. There had been no sun that day and it was already dark, flurries of snow whirling round the bare stone pillars. In better days, geraniums trailed down from baskets there. But these were not better days and the baskets had been unhooked long ago. He was carrying a leather suitcase, brand new, ridiculously small, like something a child would take on holiday. Blotches of damp from snowflakes were dotted over it. Lucy stayed in the kitchen, exchanging nervous glances with Pia as Albert hurried him across the hall. Their voices were suddenly shut off by the closing of a door.

It was days before she saw him again. He seemed embarrassed to be found. He had been walking on the little patch of dead ground hidden behind Albert's studio, smoking one of his perfumed cigarettes. She remembered that shy look from years ago when she'd seen him first, taking shelter in a little gallery on the coast. No, not exactly shy: more hunted, now. Older, of course, and thinner in the face, but something else, more subtle. It seemed he could not look at you: eyes endlessly darting nervously to the ends of his fingers, to his cigarette, never to yours. She thought less of him for this furtive wariness, it was vaguely demeaning.

But after their first encounter he seemed content for her to visit his secret place. Most of the time he sat on a bench under the big tree. The same tree she had decided not worth painting a lifetime ago, when she was very young and the worth of things seemed to matter. When the winter light was unusually clear he would creep out like some small grey animal to settle, dabbing watercolour on a piece of board on his knee. She would perch quietly on the arm of the bench to watch. She had never expected to see him work. He seemed not to mind her silent surveillance. One afternoon, she realised he had been speaking, almost whispering to himself. 'You know why I don't like people watching me?' He was looking up at her, a timid smile softening his face, seeing her embarrassment. 'No, it's alright, I make exceptions.'

'I'm sorry. You know how mothers always say it's rude to stare … well mine did. It's funny, I can't stand it either. People looking over my shoulder, I'm exactly the same. I don't know why.' Thinking of Emily in the tiled studio she felt her face grow red. She was never one for lies.

'Oh, don't you know why? For me, if I think of someone as I work they end up in the paint. Sometimes that happens. But if they are really there … well … they end up in the painting for sure. It's a risk isn't it?' He was laughing now. Perhaps laughing at her. There was something dreadful about this bleak face cracking open to laugh. 'That's why I tell people to keep away. They risk being burned.' As he wiped his eyes he saw the pity in her face and she thought he hated her for it. Speaking faster now, his careful English deserting him, pulling at her hand, hanging on to it, 'Let me tell you a story. That's what old men do … we old Jews, as they say. Do you know why do I sign my work JZ? Did you never want to know?'

'I always thought it was for the angles. You like angles.'

He leaned back, disarmed, still holding her hand, turning it over palm up. 'You're a clever thing. Maybe too clever - like Albert. You do good work … I like what you do ... but you're wrong. Here … hold it … it was my father's …' He had put his tiny cigarette lighter in her hand. A worn silver thing, surprisingly heavy. She had seen it a hundred times.

'It's a Zippo. It still works. I was only a little boy, you see. And I had sold a painting. My first. A little boy, happy seeing his father proud. What did I know about painting? The man asked me to sign it. So I signed it Zippo, after my father's lighter. Perhaps I hoped he'd give it me. Jules Zippo … I had a friend called Jules. I suppose it was a joke. But you're right, it made a shape I liked. Perhaps you're right after all.'

Before she could say anything, the sound of a car scrunching onto the gravel sent him scuttling indoors to find the narrow wooden staircase to his room. He did not wait to gather his things together and she rescued the abandoned scrap of board. The colours were only a hint away from nothing.

It had been the doctor's car. He bustled in, nodding to Albert and pausing to kiss Lucy before making his way to the fireplace, stooping to warm his hands. Since he said nothing she made to go but he waved her back.

'No, you'd better hear this.' He was speaking French, almost a whisper. Albert moved closer, cupping a hand round his ear.

'Two men came to the Mairie yesterday. We were shut actually but they banged at the door. No, it's alright, not Germans. We don't seem to merit Germans – too small I suppose. A couple of policemen. Not from round here and not very friendly. They read me a little homily, a lot of nonsense about the New France. They asked for the population list. I told them it's years out of date and they'd be better off looking at the church records. Not the right thing to say. I got another lecture, this one about laxity. Then they gave me these. It's a sort of census.'

He laid out a few sheets of cheap paper, stamped with a swastika in black ink next to the familiar RF. You couldn't help thinking it must have been a lot of work stamping each one separately.

Albert took them off him and grimaced. 'But we've already done all this. A chap came a few weeks past.' He winked at Lucy. 'One thing I do like about bureaucracies – they lose things. You can rely on it. We'll get it done tomorrow.' He fetched a glass from the dresser and pushed the brandy bottle across the table towards the doctor.

He shook his head. 'I don't think I'm explaining very well. These two knew all about the other man. We're to ignore him … no, it's not a joke, Albert. They intend to verify the records house by house. I don't like it. There's something nasty about the way these two looked. Best to get it right.' He glanced at the door. 'What I mean is, they want a list of everybody.'

A log rolled over and briefly flared into life, the tiny sound startling Lucy. The room was suddenly very quiet.

'You mean Pia?' Albert had poured himself a drink and sat looking through the amber liquid, one eye closed, lining up the other on the earnest face in front of him. He went on looking until the doctor let his gaze fall.

'Yes, there's Pia of course … they say they want everybody.'

Lucy looked up and was about to speak but Albert reached out and put a hand on top of hers. She sat on, red with shame as the gesture seemed to erase a lifetime of friendship between these two men, a lifetime of mutual confidence.

Albert carefully put his glass down and nudged it across the table like a chess piece. 'I see. Well, if they want everybody, that's easy enough. We're just the three.'

'There's another thing,' the doctor was looking at Lucy now, suddenly embarrassed. 'They're not from here. All the same, you'd never pass for French, you know that. Just try not to say much … when they come back, I mean.' He paused, tracing a joint in the tiles with his foot, thinking how to finish things. 'It must be a lonely sort of life here.' He forced an unhappy smile. 'With just the three of you, I mean.'

'We're alright. Just the three of us.'

He stood up, gathering papers together. 'No, I don't have time for a drink. I don't suppose these forms are all that important. I'll leave them with you. Just something new to get used to I expect.'

CHAPTER 8

The day the men came there was a hard frost everywhere. The first of the year. There seemed no point lighting the stove in the studio so Lucy huddled over the kitchen fire, sipping a tisane made from the last of the vervain leaves. They had fallen into the habit of making a tiny breakfast for themselves. Pia was still in bed. With the end of daily bread she had lost heart and spent longer and longer in her own room. Occasionally, unaccustomed footsteps shuffled over the wooden boards overhead as she moved about. Occasionally, they heard her pulling out drawers. But mostly she slept. Around midday, Lucy made a sort of porridge for them all, carrying the steaming plate across the hall and up to Pia's room.

The first of the policemen opened the kitchen door without knocking and stood on the terrace outside, letting cold air flood into the room. A second man stayed on the terrace. Beyond him, a soldier leaned against the half-open door of the car, a rifle propped beside him. He was smoking a cigarette.

Albert began to close the door, but the man tugged at his arm and pushed him back. 'Leave it. This won't take long.'

They were speaking French. Lucy could not identify the accent. She drew closer to the fireplace, her heart pounding, and poked a log with her toe.

'Pia Berri. That you?' The man was staring at her, looking up from a sheaf of paper. When she didn't reply he shrugged and looked at Albert, waving the bundle in her direction.

'Pia's upstairs. She's our cook. She's not well – I'll see if she can come down.'

'Sit down grandpa, we don't have all day. You take me.' This to Lucy, who pulled her coat tight round her shoulders and led the way across the freezing hall and up the staircase. She heard the man clattering behind, trying to keep up. She paused at Pia's door, about to knock, but the man barged past, swinging the door wide, letting it bang against the wall. Pia was sitting up in bed, blankets tight round her shoulders, her face tiny under a green woollen hat. She gave them a sullen stare, inching herself a little higher against the pillows.

'Pia Berri?' She nodded. 'Cook?' There was the hint of a sneer in his voice. She nodded wearily, black eyes darting questions to Lucy as the man went on writing.

Going downstairs he paused in front of one of Albert's paintings, blocking her way. He stood looking then nodded down the stairs, 'Albert Bradley, painter - that'll be him then?' Lucy nodded and stood head bowed waiting for him to move.

'Talkative, aren't you? God, it's cold here.' He almost ran back down taking the stairs two at a time. When she reached the kitchen he was waiting for her.

'Lucile Beyrou?' She nodded. 'Artist?' The sarcasm was inescapable. Lucy stooped down by the fire and mumbled yes, letting the word turn into a cough. Albert glanced nervously across but he went on writing. His companion had been fidgeting with the door catch and looked up as the man called his name, laughing. 'That's what it's called, Thierry – "Artist" - remember if the missus asks.' Suddenly serious, he snarled at Albert. 'She's young enough to be your granddaughter for Christ's sake. What a place. You must be mad.'

He stacked the forms into a cardboard box, squeezing the lid shut. 'These will be checked. You'll get them back … tomorrow.' They heard the other man snigger. 'Well, tomorrow's another day, isn't that what they say? Don't you worry, you'll get them back. You'll need them.' He showed no signs of going, edging closer to the fire, standing with his leg pressed against Lucy's chair. 'Damned cold here. I don't know how you stand it.' He was looking at the brandy bottle on the table. Albert picked up the newspaper and folded it back.

As they went, the man pushed the door hard against the wall as far as it would go and left it that way. Lucy suddenly felt helplessly vulnerable. The car scrunched across the gravel, cutting an insolent scar into the edge of the lawn.

'Push the door to, will you Poppy, dear? I need a drink.'

'I think we both do.' Tears had started into her eyes hearing the old name.

'Don't you go doing that, my girl. They're just a couple of jumped up busybodies. Mind you, I didn't like the look of that soldier. Thank God you didn't have much to say. I'll have a good listen tomorrow and see whether we can do something about it. Trouble is, that rail pass thing says you come from Clermond, although Lucile didn't have that accent. D'you think you could manage being Belgian? What about that? What do you know about Belgium?'

The question was so absurd Lucy started a choking sort of laugh, struggling to stop. 'You're nice, you know. Did I mention that?'

'Any reason in particular?'

'You know perfectly well.'

Of course, nobody brought the forms back. No great inconvenience, at least until the grocer's cards were filled up and there was no way of replacing them. Then there was no choice but to join the long queue at the Mairie, shuffling forward inch by inch in a wet brown slush of half-melted snow. The old brass plaque had been stuck over with red paper swastikas. There were swastikas everywhere, pasted on shop windows, pinned incongruously to the church door, even in a few windows. The first day they waited all morning, watching the sun move through a clear sky the colour of water, nudging each other sullenly forward like cattle penned in a slaughter yard, until the doors slammed, a young soldier in grey uniform managing the word, "Demain" in an odd accent, smirking as the line unfolded into little knots of cowed old women.

They got the papers on the third day. At first, a man in steel spectacles took Pia's out of the envelope and snapped, "In person," but a squat woman sitting behind a desk, opening and closing wooden file drawers, leaned over and said it was alright, she was her aunt. The spectacles stared for a moment, looked wearily at the line snaking along the road, and put the form back into the envelope.

Not that it mattered much because Pia left soon afterwards. Her sister kept goats and her house was smaller. It would only be for a day or two until she found her feet. She would be able to bring them milk. She never returned. Albert moved his things into the kitchen and set up an easel within range of the fire. Lucy's huge canvas stayed where it was, silent and frozen upstairs. Life fell into its own grim routine: lighting the fire, the terrible walk to the village looking for bread, a single meal of whatever could be bought or stolen. Brandy mixed with water.

Thinking of their secret Jew, as night fell Albert hoisted a blanket over the window each evening, but Paul came down to join them less and less. He was sleeping in Albert's old studio, a tiny paraffin heater filling the room with fumes but little heat. He ate whatever they gave him in silence, holding his plate in gloved hands, masticating slowly, looking at them, a look almost of pity.

One evening he came into the kitchen and asked Albert for a cigarette. 'I miss my cigarettes. I regret the way I went through them. I could have rationed myself, but you never think, do you?' Albert shook his head, shoving the box of little cigars across the table. He took one and lit it carefully. 'I saw a little of the last war, not the fighting you understand, I wasn't a soldier. Even then it seemed pointless, although best not to say so. It looks like they are going to starve us this time.'

Lucy thought how quickly you fall into a way of talking. Even about things impossibly strange. She looked at him and murmured, 'Who are they? Do you know? When you say "they" – is there a they?'

'I suppose not.' He looked at her, rheumy eyes filmed milky white. How old he looks, you would not credit his falling away so fast. He glanced at the door then, remembering Pia was not there, gave a sick kind of grin. 'I'm not going to Madagascar you know. Too old for one thing.'

'Me neither.' Albert paused, the brandy bottle hovering over Paul's glass. 'I'm not even sure I know where it is. Is this a new parlour game? Places we're not going to.'

'I remember my father talking about Madagascar when I was a child. Just a little boy. He read it out to all of us. Somebody had written a letter to the newspaper suggesting the Jews should have their own country. Well, perhaps not their own, but something like that. Somewhere to put them. Elsewhere, anyway. It's French, you know … a colony … I suppose it's German now. Odd to think that's how it's done. You wonder if they know – the Madagascans, I mean?' He drew on the little cigar and started to cough. Lucy brought him a glass of water. 'Apparently we are to go to Madagascar again. You weren't listening. It was on the wireless.'

It was the first time Lucy had heard him say "we" like that. Before, it was always "the Jews" or "Jewish people". Now it was "we".

'Something else. A cloth star; to be sewn on all outer garments. Yellow. The dimensions are in the newspaper, so they say. Do you think you can get a newspaper?'

It sounded so ludicrous Lucy burst out laughing. 'It's a joke. Surely some sort of German joke. Do Germans have jokes? It's completely mad.'

'No, I don't think it's a joke. Anyway, it would have to be a French joke, wouldn't it? This star is a French idea. You didn't get a letter about it because there are no Jews here. I don't exist. As you know.' He was smiling to himself. 'It is a relief, this not existing, because I shall not comply.'

Albert turned uncomfortably in his chair, embarrassed. 'I saw one in the village. I remember thinking it queer. That day I went for meat – not that there was any, just a few bits of gristle. Quite a young chap. He came out of that place where you get the ration cards. He'd sewn it on his overcoat. They were taking it out on him, pushing him out of the shop. J-P says it's going to be a problem. He had to do the list of Jews. You don't get cards unless you're French and the bloke in charge keeps saying he has to confirm you can be both - French and Jewish. J-P says he's at his wits' end not knowing what do.'

'He'll get used to it.' The bitterness was impossible to ignore. 'It's suddenly awkward being a Jew. I'd never thought about it before. I should have, but then many of my friends are Jewish. You might say they would be. Artists, you see. A bad influence on the young - you should know that Poppy ... you remember that? Is it because we are artists or because we are Jews? Who's to say? But I know this much – our new France doesn't have much time for painting.' He carefully pinched the cigar out and got up. 'Thanks for this - I'll eke it out a bit at a time.'

Eventually they stopped having breakfast together. Coffee had long since run out and it seemed pointless to congregate round an empty table with nothing to do. Lucy would boil a little water and pour it over mashed up sprigs of wild thyme, the resinous smell rising with the steam. She made enough for three and left it in the saucepan. It served well enough to dampen stale bread. On Sundays, Albert opened a tin: ham or corned beef. Pia's immaculate larder was still stocked with rows of tins, mostly luxuries from another age. A tin rarely lasted beyond the middle of the week.

One Wednesday morning Albert was dribbling brandy into a pot of porridge made from oatmeal. The two of them were alone.

'Paul's late again,' he sounded irritable.

Lucy was in no mood to go looking for him. For one thing she had stomach ache – the usual low dragging pain, although there was no blood now. She seemed to have none to give. And she had woken to find a tooth loose. She tried to inspect it in the bathroom mirror and found a gaunt face staring back at her, skin unnaturally tight round the eyes, the mouth oddly swollen, teeth pushing the jaw out, framing it like a half-formed skull. The tooth had wobbled slightly in its socket and she had flinched at a sharp jab of pain, a flush of panic seizing her. She never thought her teeth might betray her. They were coming loose one by one. She was dying. Bit by bit, starving – all of them. That was the way of it. No fighting, no guns, no soldiers, no crowds - just people huddled in houses slowly starving. That was how it would be: as quiet as the grave. She watched Albert clumsily stirring his pan, his back to her, stooping to breathe in the vapours of brandy. In their mutual misery she had stopped looking at him. Something about the scrawny flesh of his neck rising thin from his collar brought tears to her eyes. She went to the door and stood for a second holding the catch. 'You go on stirring your stuff, I'll get him. He'll be still asleep. Go easy on that brandy.'

He turned to look at her and for a second seemed almost angry. 'Why? The cellar's full of brandy. We must have enough to see out a couple of wars. Mind you, how do you know when a war's over? D'you think somebody will tell us? We're not at war with anybody – we're just being left to rot.'

'I'll go and call him. Try and get the fire going a bit. It's cold in here.'

She went across the hall and stood listening at the foot of the silent staircase. A dreadful chill filled the place, not damp, but harsh and dry. Her breath hung in a fine cloud of mist. It was almost too cold to breathe. She did not call. There seemed no point and in any case she never knew quite what to call him, so she laboured her way to the floor above, past her own room, and up the second flight of stairs.

The studio door was closed. There was no sound. A card was pinned to the door, perfectly square, very neat. He had drawn on it a double intersecting triangle forming a star, the lines miraculously sharp, the thing washed over with yellow watercolour. He's faded it with grey, she thought, funny how he could never bring himself to use strong colour. Angles made by the intersecting lines collided, giving the image the strangely disturbing quality of something unreal floating over the surface of the card. He always liked angles.

As she pushed the door open she knew what she would find. She had known really since Albert had spoken. Both of them had known. That's why he had not turned round; why he was angry. He hadn't wanted to come; not up here. What had she expected? It had been in her mind even as she climbed the stairs.

But there was no body, no swinging shadow, no hanging thing; although he was surely gone. No horror, just an old man doubled forward in a chair, his head almost cradled in his lap. She saw the thin hairs on the back of his neck and a surge of fury filled her. Why should it come to this? He had done his share for humanity, more than his share. His paintings said more than these new barbarians wanted to know. But they knew enough to fear them; knew enough to rip them down; to burn them. She kneeled to look into his closed eyes, daring to touch his chin, feeling the stubble cold against her hand.

It must have been 'flu, although he had said nothing. He had eaten little for days. Stuck up here on his own what did he do with himself? Lucy looked round the studio, unchanged from years ago when she had worked here herself. She had painted *Figures on a Lawn* on that easel propped against the far wall. He had placed a little table near the window. That must be where he worked. He was always neat, you could say that. He had even found a neat way of dying. She stood looking down at the shrunken figure wondering why tears refused to come. But horror was now so much a part of life that tears seemed too great a concession.

Albert's footsteps were heavy on the stairs; he was standing in the doorway, breathing hard, unwilling to come further. He did not speak.

'He was like this when I found him.'

He came over then, gently pushing the old man back into his chair. 'Poor chap … he was a good friend to me. To you too. What the hell's all this about?' He was staring at her as if he almost expected a reply, bright blue eyes filled with tears. 'This nonsense had nothing to do with him, nothing at all. He was a painter, for God's sake. And a bloody good one. One of the best. Wouldn't hurt a fly.' He was beating a bunched fist into his other hand, the catch in his voice made Lucy look away. She went across to Paul's table, shuffling papers together, running her finger along tubes of paint neatly set out in lines. He was always neat. On the other side of the table there was a frame on its side, loosely covered with a blue cloth. He must have been sitting in this tall chair to paint, the paraffin heater pressed hard against his legs.

Albert reached it first. He lifted the cloth and leaned down over the canvas. It was small, only a few feet across. From where she stood, Lucy could make no sense of the diagonal lines jostling against each other. She glanced at Albert. He was standing quite still, an expression on his face she had never seen before. Something close to fear.

'What's the matter?'

It was some time before he spoke. 'You can't see it from there. Come round here.'

She shuffled round the table and looked at the pattern of lines. They looked like teeth. What were they? 'But he never painted figures … did he?'

'Oh yes, when he was young - all the time. Blissful things. He could draw like Holbein, you know. You've only seen his later stuff.' Albert gently picked the frame up and propped it against a pile of books.

The shock when she stepped back was like a physical blow. She could see it for what it was: something almost a face, livid yellow, larger than the canvas, its monstrous mouth open, teeth stepped back in serried lines like white lances readied for some dreadful battle. As she saw how he had made this miracle work, how you could be inside and outside a horror at the same time, part of her could not help saying clever devil. The dreadful mask of the picture seemed to violate her, filling her head with a familiar terror – a terror that had lived with her always. How had he known that?

'Clever devil,' murmured Albert, 'clever old devil.'

This was not some agonised plea for mercy; not some awful soundless scream; nothing of the pity of suffering, nothing of war. None of those things. This face was waiting for some fragment of time to pass. And waiting, you must wait with it. As she struggled not to look, the dreadful thing turned round on itself, as she knew it would, and Lucy realised she was looking through it, gazing out on a dark world.

'He's signed it.' Albert was running a finger along the line of tacks on the frame. 'He only signed things he'd finished.' He looked across at the silent figure slumped in its chair. Paul might have been asleep. The mouth was open, a small dribble of something white running down his chin.

CHAPTER 9

In the New France you needed permission to die.

Albert had brought a crumpled buff form back from the Mairie. It had been pouring with rain all day. He sat at the kitchen table easing his shoes off and pushing them to steam in front of the fire.

'J-P was upset. I've never seen him that way. Says I should have confided in him, told him we had Paul here. Said he could have helped. Got in a dreadful stew about us not trusting him. I told him to leave you out of it, and what was I supposed to do, anyway? I'd no right to pile our problem on his shoulders - he's got problems enough. And why the hell is Paul a problem? Why did I say that?'

He caught the look in her face and blazed up at her, 'For God's sake don't you go taking pity on me. Anything but that. Look, I'll tell you something. I wasn't going to, but now I will. He's got this poster on the wall. He stood there while I read it. It says you're shot for harbouring Jews. Full of spelling mistakes, I may add, they don't care much for the language. But I suppose that's what we were doing, *harbouring*, even if the bastards can't spell it.'

She had never seen him so worked up, as if something had broken inside him. He was never angry. Well, perhaps when you looked the wrong way at a painting that hadn't worked. But those were just summer storms and never lasted. Now, he was white with fury. He could barely keep still. He shambled over to the window in stockinged feet and stood staring out at the bare chestnut tree, his back heaving, trying to calm himself. She looked at him and for a second was on *Malapet* again, with Laura. When was it? A dozen years ago or more; neither of them knowing what to do with him in that incredible heatwave. The way she felt, having to touch his face for the first time; a grown-up's face – you don't forget that. Sponging his head bright red with the fever, water dripping everywhere.

Albert turned, as if he knew what she was thinking and shrugged. 'I must have been in that office hundreds of times. I used to play chess there with his father when he was alive. Seeing that poster stuck there. Obscene really – like finding somebody had scrawled dirty words on the wall. The things kids do. I asked him what it meant exactly, *harbouring*? And why the hell he'd let them stick it up? You know what he said? He said, "If I take it down they'll shoot me." I thought he was going to cry, poor chap. I think that's what decided me. Right then.'

But he didn't say what he had decided, just went on staring beyond the chestnut tree to the dark band of trees marking the edge of the lawn. When they were children that forest was where you ran away. They all believed nobody would ever find you in there; that was the comfort of it. You could run for ever in those woods.

The rain had stopped, a violet sky closing over the trees. They knew so little of this war. A kind of agreement had grown between them that they would know as little as they could. Painting would be enough for both of them until the madness ended. It showed no sign of ending, but they never talked about it, simply losing interest in the little orange light and its endless posturing lectures. Painting made more sense, or at least a sort of sense. They passed their days, each of them, in other worlds: each dimly aware *something* was happening, each content enough that it was all a long way off.

But they were very hungry.

Albert had sat down and pulled the oil lamp across the table looking at the form lying there, idly ironing out the damp creases with his thumbnail.

'J-P says people have stopped asking for him to come out to them. It's not a doctor they need, it's something decent to eat. They say they don't want to bother him. Impressive, if you think about it, given nobody's got anything to eat, including him. Now they only come to register the deaths. Pretty well every day. He says all the old ones are dying off. They catch something and that's that. Like with Paul. The Prefect's on his back all the time to keep the records up to date. The death records. He showed me a letter telling him the New France doesn't accept laxity in record keeping. If it wasn't so grim, you'd laugh. It's driving him mad.'

'I think it's driving me mad as well, Albert. It's started that I don't think about anything else. I can't work. I thought painting would let me escape, but I'm too soft I suppose. I can't bear being hungry all the time. How did it get this way? You should change into something dry. What if you go catching something? It's the old ones that go first - you said it yourself.'

She had been trying to smile when she said it but he grabbed her by the arm, 'You're not following me, my girl, not following at all. The point is, his records are a complete mess, don't you see? And there's no church records at all - they've stopped them. You see what I mean? You see? He's got a collection of spare dead people.' Lucy was frowning, about to say something, but he raised a hand. 'No, best you don't go asking that. What he's given me will do for Paul, that's all that matters.' He took a battered card out of an envelope and peered at it. 'The poor chap's going to be buried as Ignace Berek, profession agriculteur, age 83, cause of death constitutional weakness. That should do. We're to say he worked in the garden here if anybody asks. But nobody will - too many burials to bother with questions. The hearse is coming at six in the morning. J-P's donating the fuel.'

'I don't think I can bear a funeral. Do you mind?'

'It's alright – there isn't one. They've stopped having them since the priest got himself locked up. Those two Alsatian policemen turned up and told him he needed a licence to organise a cult. He didn't know what they were on about. You've seen him: he's the ancient chap in the cassock wandering around like the Abbé Constatin. He's been here for ever; he looks too old to die. Anyway, he gave them an argument, said he'd never heard anything so stupid. So they arrested him. He's alright, J-P has seen him. But they're keeping him there until he signs something and he says he won't. You know, Lucy, I think everybody's gone insane. No, you stay behind. Keep warm. I'll see Paul's buried alright. And don't you worry about the name. He was funny about names. After all that JZ stuff, he'll see the funny side of it.'

He went through into the salon and you could hear him tugging at drawers. He came back carrying a stiff manila envelope. 'We'd better bury this tomorrow, in the garden. It's his papers, what I can find of them. They were in that little suitcase. I'll put them in a tin. We two are the only ones to know where he is, so you'd better remember.'

She slept little that night, wondering what Albert meant when he said he'd decided something. He would tell her eventually. He was like that: you could never get anything out of him just by asking. The wind in the trees was keeping her awake. It always did that. There had been wind in the roof the day she tried to copy that little painting of Paul's. She remembered how she felt discovering he'd fixed it for her: corrected it. Signed it, what's more. The first time she'd seen that peculiar J looped round the letter Z. She really hadn't been the same since then; become permanently different. All Paul's doing, God bless him wherever he is. Not that he was very keen on God. Maybe exceptions can be made. Paul with his scented cigarettes. Charming, immaculate, patient, Paul with his white cotton gloves and his patent leather shoes. You would never guess he saw things nobody had ever seen, not even Leonardo – really, none of them. You would not have thought it to look at him. People daubing on cave walls, on skins, paper, canvas, anything, just so things could endure, to keep *timor mortis* at bay a few more days. Until Paul, who wasn't interested in things at all. Paul, the quiet little man with kind eyes who discovered how to paint ideas. Paul, who painted thoughts - which is not at all nice, when you got down to it. They were burning them even now: his paintings. He'd told her the day he arrived the Paris ones had gone already. Chucked out of a window by a couple of leering idiots. He'd kept some nonsense in a letter to *Le Figaro* folded in his wallet. *Degenerate,* that was the word. Paul seemed unconcerned. Sensible really, because burning was completely pointless. Once thoughts were out, where would you propose putting them back? No wonder they wanted to burn his stuff. The rain had started again. She lay on her back, listening to the rattle on the window panes, hoping they would burn hers too. That would be worth something. It was then she thought of the painting he had left for them. Nobody was going to burn that.

Since Pia had left, they didn't bother with shutters. She could hear them rattling against the walls outside as she ran along the dark of the corridor to Paul's studio. The painting was where they'd left it, shards of glistening white running into the dark. Albert was right, it really was a dreadful thing. She gathered it up in its cloth and scuttled back to her bedroom. She would hide it somewhere in the studio tomorrow. There were dozens of canvases stacked in there and she would slide it amongst them. Albert would know what to do. Nobody was going to burn it. She fell asleep wondering what it was he had decided.

She had been dreaming of Oscar when the car bumping across the gravel drive woke her: the car taking Paul away. She thought how she used to bring his breakfast to him. She would never see him again. It seemed for a moment they had taken Oscar with them and she felt desolate. It was unfair: dreams of Oscar were never happy. Even when reality set no constraints, somehow they were always unsatisfactory. Years ago as a little girl she had rubbed herself to sleep resolved to dream of Oscar lying alongside her. But it had never been so. Sleep offered only anxious dreams of meetings that never occurred, preparations never fruitful, things forgotten. Once – just once – they had come close and something fierce and dangerous had woken her in the dark, her heart racing, sweating with panic.

The lamp was still burning in the kitchen when she went down. He had left it for her. The room seemed so bright you felt light-headed, unnaturally alert in the empty house, the wind across the terrace outside filling the place with small night sounds. Beyond a mist of drizzle on the windows, a grudging grey dawn was starting. She saw to the fire but it had barely caught when she heard the car return. There was something unbearable about how little time it had all taken.

J-P would not come in. She wrapped a blanket round Albert's shoulders and steered him to the fire, his face white with the chill. He said nothing about Paul. Perhaps he never would, keeping it as something between the two of them. Two old men, seeing to things. She didn't mind; it was an end to something. They toasted the last of the bread at the fire and made a breakfast of sardines. Paul deserved the best they had. Albert filled a glass of brandy and sat glaring silently into the flames. At least, there was still plenty of brandy.

A week later, she reached the grocers to discover cabbages everywhere, the shop full of them. The scramble to get inside had ended in a fierce silent wedge of determined women at the narrow door. She had been too weary with the walk to do more than let herself be jostled to the back, an old man with a stick hanging on to her. The place was filled with piles of coarse green dimpled leaves splattered with clay soil. Some were stacked on the counter; mostly they were all over the floor, spilling out of cardboard trays, filling the place with a raw unhealthy smell of wet earth. As the need to fight evaporated, the mood changed a little and those who had made it to the front relaxed. There were even cautious smiles as neighbours dared recognise each other. One by one they shuffled forward holding out bank notes that the succeeding weeks had made increasingly pointless. Cabbages were handed over the counter. Some were even passed along the line in an echo of ancient bread shop courtesies, long since abandoned.

As the damp weight of the cabbage was pushed into her hands, a squat woman with a baby at her breast prodded her in the back. She was one of the new people from the town who had been moved into the Post Office. Nobody had seen any of them before. Rumour had it they spent most of their time opening letters and making copies, but it was best not to believe everything you heard. Some rumours were now so disgusting you were ashamed to hear them at all, ashamed to give them space in your head. In the Post Office you could never get this woman even to say good morning. Now she was almost smiling: an unpleasant lopsided grimace showing bad teeth. 'You're from the big house, aren't you? You've a letter come. It's for him. The painter. You'll get it at the Office.' She looked vaguely unhappy, staring at the press of listening women, challenging them to deny it if they liked.

The boy behind the counter didn't want to tick her card. He handed it back. Cabbages didn't count – not when the place was full of them.

Outside on the pavement, something made her glance back over the heads of the queue. The same woman with the baby was pulling at the shirt of a boy at her side. She had not noticed him before. Undernourished and lanky, he was stooping the way children did now, bent forward as if he had stomach ache. He tugged the shirt irritably back out of his mother's hand and straightened up, sunken black eyes in a face white as plaster dust. He was not very old, but it was hard to tell: fourteen, perhaps. For an unfortunate second their eyes met and she looked away, embarrassed.

The Post Office was not closed but the place was empty. A black and white swastika sagged down from an upstairs window alongside the old French flag. Inside, a huge poster stuck onto the grille over the counter proclaimed, WATCH YOUR WALLET in garish red, the background a crude caricature of a hook-nosed Fagin. There was no point even calling out; the place was obviously deserted. On the other side of the grille the door to the back office was wide open, a metal table covered with mail sacks. As she went outside the thought of the long walk back was almost too much to bear. The white-faced youth was walking up the street. When he saw her he stopped, leaning against the wall, waiting for her to pass.

There was no reason to be frightened, no reason at all, but the panic was there nonetheless: immediate and shocking. The lanky boy, for he really was no more than a boy, looked harmless enough, leaning against the wall, pretending to catch his breath. But he had no reason to be here - the road was a dead end - no reason at all, unless he was going to the Post Office. In which case, why lean against the wall? He had followed her from the shop, there was no getting away from it. She could see all the way down the deserted lane, narrow houses on each side shuttered and dumb. To get back she had to walk past him and, idiotically, it was already too late to do that. He had seen her stop; he had seen her hesitate, seen the desperate glance back; he had seen her look for a way of escape. There was something absurd and horrible about this: by stopping, she had imprisoned herself.

There was nothing to do but stand immobile, staring pointlessly down the street, hoping for someone to come, letting a chill of terror seep up. She had often wondered what it would be like to be trapped. What it would be like to be attacked. The problem was you never knew how it might happen, except that it would happen at the most innocent of times. It would happen when your guard was down, when you had no call to guard, in moments free from peril. Then it would come, and you would realise just too late. And it was all true. She had never imagined it would be today. Her heart was thumping now. Her greatest fear was to be smothered. Was it going to come to that? Pinned down, powerless, struggling to breathe. Could he do that? Would she fight? She tried to imagine fighting, but knowing he was there looking back at her meant the thought would not come. He was idly kicking his feet against the pavement, a relentless soft scraping noise. Why was he there? He was waiting for someone and she was the only person here. She stared at him, her eyes burning. He was still leaning against the wall, looking at his feet, scuffing them against a doorstep; waiting. The Post Office behind her was further away than she realised, much further. And as she ran, a movement followed, little boy's pattering feet, faster than hers. He seemed not to be running but was catching her. Soon he would be alongside. Holding her cabbage awkwardly in both hands, stumbling up the steps, almost falling into the dry papery smell of the empty Post Office. Too late to shove at the door, he had reached it as she felt the counter at her back. He was inside, glancing up at the red poster, startled. Really no more than a boy, but too close. He drew a rattle of phlegm into his throat and swallowed. For a second there was a fleeting expression on his face, something like exasperation, as if he had been put to some unnecessary inconvenience. He lunged forward, clumsily wrenching the cabbage from her hands, and ran out into the street. By the time she followed, he had gone.

Later that night as she poured out this story to Albert she did not even notice she was weeping tears of humiliation. Now she thought about it, the daily walk to the village had become a torment. She shouldn't have to rest like that every few yards, hunched up like an old woman by the roadside, leaning down to catch her breath. Something was going wrong with her. What was the point if anything you managed to buy was wiped out by the effort of getting it? When it hadn't seemed serious – when the war, whatever that meant, seemed no more than a complicated jumble of unconnected events - money had tipped the scales.

They had enough of that, after all; although you had to be careful. People hate you for being rich, even when it's not your fault. People in the shop hated them, she knew that, but took their money, all the same. Even when the price asked was insane, they took the money. Now, money didn't come into it. Money had stopped. Money was a waste of time.

Knowing she never wept, she let tears run down her face, stammering out her story, realising the affair with the cabbage had settled something. Weeping for the hopelessness of it all. How it was going to end. Weeping for Albert as well, Albert most of all, because he didn't deserve this. Nobody cared about them, that was the truth. And why should they? Why should they give a damn about an old man they didn't know and a feeble foreign girl? What did they know about either of them? She realised she had stopped talking, silently bunching a handkerchief in her hand.

Albert was standing behind her, his hand stretched out over her head, hesitating to touch her shoulder, like someone uncertain how best to wake a sleeping body. 'You were miles away. Something I wanted to talk about, if you're up to it.'

'I can't talk. It's just not worth trying to walk up there anymore, it's really not. I don't think I can, not after today. You as well - it's too far. That hill is too much. I know he didn't mean anything, he probably just wanted the cabbage, but it made me see how they all felt. They want us to keep away. We're not part of them, never will be. We'll just have to stay here.'

The calm in his face was a surprise and, mistaking the reason, she felt suddenly angry. He hadn't understood a word. There was something infuriating about his unconcern. She struggled on, desperate, 'After all there's some food here. Tinned stuff. Plenty of it. The mistake's been trying to spin everything out. We've just ended up too weak to think. At least we can eat without walking for it. It should last until the weather gets better.'

'Then what?'

That same mock solemn look in his face. He obviously hadn't meant it to sound like a challenge, but she hung her head, silently biting her lip. Night sounds had started up outside; an owl screeching. He knew what she meant. They had trapped themselves staying here. She should have got out when Oscar said. The business with the cabbage had made her see she was incomplete in some way. The truth of it was she couldn't cope. All she was fit for was painting and that is not really a life. It was not enough.

'I suppose we can see what's in the garden. We can look. And we can plant things ...' She was faltering, fighting a hysterical desire to laugh. God, even death was going to make a fool of her. Why bother? He knew what she meant; he always knew what she was thinking. Paul had decided to give up. That was what he had done and she could do the same. Now she had embraced the thought, the sleepy inevitability of it didn't seem so very terrible. But the thought of Albert watering tomatoes taunted her like some final insanity. Albert pottering about in his smock. She put a hand to her mouth, biting her fingers for the hurt of it, warding off the hysterical desire to laugh.

'I said, how long? How long do you think?' He was looking away, letting her compose herself, trying to help, his voice little more than a growl. 'This business with the larder: how long do you reckon the stuff will last? Have you looked? Look Poppy, I told you, I've made my mind up. I want to talk about it.'

'You shouldn't call me that, you know you shouldn't. You'll go and forget one day and then where will we be? I'm not asking you to do anything. I've made up my mind.' She couldn't help it, she was sobbing again, hating herself for the futility of it. 'I'm just not scrabbling for cabbages any more ... I'm not ... I can't. I must be made of the wrong stuff. Too sensitive or something. I can't manage. I'd rather sit here and go to sleep. That's not such a terrible thing.'

'I'll get you a drink. You didn't tell me about the letter.'

'I knew you weren't listening. I told you, there wasn't one. Don't you see? There was nothing. The woman said it to get me there I suppose. It was just a trick. There wasn't a letter.'

'I have to tell you about that letter.'

CHAPTER 10

So that was the day she learned war was about lies; above all else, it was about lies. And since lies breed lies, nothing from then on in her life was certainly true. Which was, of course, a comfort. England had not lost: that had been a lie. Certainly, England seemed in a perpetual state of losing, but she had not lost; not yet. And the comfort of knowing Oscar was in England and that England had not lost made even hunger a kind of consolation - if she was to perish here, at least she would perish believing something good about Oscar. It was shaming that first thoughts had not been for Mother and that Stuart, Laura and Ian took second place; but there was not enough comfort to go round – that was the truth of it. Along with England, Oscar had not lost: shaming or not, that was keeping her alive.

Albert began his explanation as he sat by the fire that evening, draped in a blanket, letting a few logs burn down to ash, evening sunlight colouring the room pale red. Talking about the lies of war, pressing her to follow him step by step; talking carefully as if, of a sudden, he had a special interest in all this madness. Taking such care stepping round things you wondered if this was a lie as well. Although you could say that about Albert: he didn't bother to tell lies.

It seemed the woman from the Post Office, the one with the chalk-faced boy, had wished Lucy no harm. If she had seemed wary, that was for the benefit of watching eyes. It had been, if you like, a necessary lie. The lanky boy who followed her meant no harm either. Quite the reverse, he had run after her until, being sick and hungry, he could run no longer. Albert smiled as she protested about the cabbage. Why then had he snatched the cabbage? 'He had a message for you, but you seemed hell bent on not hearing it. So, frustration, my dear, frustration … I suppose the extra cabbage was his consolation prize.' At which she sat on, feeling foolish, feeling betrayed.

He was explaining the decision he made that day in J-P's office. The day he saw the poster about harbouring Jews. He could not account for it – even now could not find the words - but pent up grief for Paul had somehow unhinged him. All the same he should have told her, he really should, because now he had drawn them both into something and they could not go back. He should have explained.

J-P had nodded at the poster and asked Albert whether he could look after somebody else, speaking quite normally, almost making a joke of it, saying given he had taken to secret harbouring, could he harbour a bit longer? There had been the hint of a grim smile, staring up at that poster, pausing a long time before saying he thought not a Jew, then adding, but not safe, not at all safe. Not looking at Albert's face, walking behind his desk, fiddling with things, leaving the question hanging in the silent room. Albert not even replying, just looking at the obscene thing on the wall, anger boiling in him, nodding his head, thoughtfully you might say, as if accepting a point in some well-rehearsed debate between old friends. All the time J-P quietly talking, head bowed, shuffling the papers on the desk.

It was not a case of one. There would be two of them, just a couple of young blokes, probably with bicycles. No knowing when they'd come, but Albert would get notice. There would be a letter: a letter that wouldn't arrive. One of the new women in the Post Office would arrange things. She had a son in a camp in Germany and had reason enough to help. It would be a case of a letter gone missing, nothing unusual these days. The best sort of message really, because it didn't exist. And safe enough even if the woman let them down, because you couldn't trust anyone. After the message, they would arrive a day or two later, maybe longer – these things were uncertain. All Albert had to do was put them up and keep them out of sight. He'd do it himself but the Mairie was filled with police most days now and it was impossible to hide someone in a doctor's surgery. Just put them up, feed them for a day or two, leave them alone. Above all, don't ask questions. Just a few days. Could he do that? Albert had laughed then, saying it didn't sound hard, apart from the feeding bit, but J-P did not smile back, just said they would bring food with them. He had been looking at the poster when he added, suddenly serious. "Not Jews, but you realise it's the same – the same risk." That was when their eyes met.

Albert was looking at her, waiting for her to say something. 'I told him I'd have to ask you. If we're going to do it, we have to do it together ... I mean, I'm getting you ... I've got you ... into something ... you do see that?' The pause was enough for her to know there was a kind of pretence in this. His decision had been days ago. The letter had already arrived, or rather had not arrived. Perhaps the men he had agreed to hide were here already. Once you start these things they have a life of their own. It was too late for persuasion; too late to turn it all back.

He was still talking, leaning forward, letting the blanket fall to lie on the floor. 'You know, when we got to the churchyard we couldn't find the hole. It was horrible, stuck there in the pitch black, mad really. Just the lights on the hearse and they weren't much use. I don't know why, but I thought somebody would be waiting for us - a grave-digger, somebody like that. We were stumbling around, tripping over gravestones and flowerpots. In the end, it was the driver who found it. Saw a spade stuck in the stuff they'd dug out. Right over the far side, by the wall. That's a terrible thing to see. The three of us got the coffin over, God knows how. Didn't know what to do then. You need ropes for a job like that and we hadn't got any.' He stopped speaking, chafing his hands, staring into the fire, his thoughts miles away. 'We got it done, but it wasn't the way it should have been. Put the earth back. He'll be alright there, Paul ... I should have taken something to leave. I forgot.' He was crying, letting tears roll down his face without embarrassment. He looked old.

'I'm sorry. I should have been there. To help. I'm a coward really. I'll take some flowers tomorrow. It's not far to walk. I don't know what he would like. He wasn't a man for flowers.'

'Better not. There are burials every day now. You can't risk it.' He stood up, rubbing his face with two enormous hands, looking directly at her. 'I feel the same as you, you know. Didn't want any part of this bloody madness, never did. But ... damn it ... how can you avoid saying but?'

He should have told her about taking the men in. It hurt to realise he had understood her so little. Although, perhaps he feared she would say no – she had that reputation. He deserved a smile for that thought. 'You should have said yes for me as well. Of course you should have said yes.'

But the men did not arrive. J-P had said a matter of two days after the message, but three uneventful days brought no one, although beds had been made and rooms swept. When the time had stretched out to a week, and then ten days, uncertainty crept in. Perhaps even this was all some complicated lie of war? Perhaps there were no visitors – they had fallen into the habit of calling them that. After two weeks it seemed certain the business was dead, leaving the fact that questions could not be asked as one more frustration. But the visitors had been sufficient excuse to begin a raid on the remains of Pia's larder. A raid, once started that was only going to end when the shelves were bare. Breakfast porridge now was sloppy with condensed milk and they gorged on the sweetness of it. The bottles of duck soup would give them a week or two of evening meals; no longer a worry, they said, because the visitors would be here before then, and the visitors were bringing food. They even began to make a modest mid-day meal of tinned meat. They both knew it - they were engaged in a reckless calculus, pitting starvation against the visitors' arrival. They both knew it and both said nothing. Sunday of the third week marked the last of the condensed milk. The visitors did not come.

Feeling a little stronger, work seemed possible again. The first of the huge canvases waited half-finished in her studio. The place was dark and stuffy. It was humiliating being almost too weak to push back the stiff shutters and let the light in. An autumn wind gusting past filled the room with the earthy scent of a false spring. That day it was not even particularly cold and the stone sill outside was sticky with damp. How many times had she leaned out of this window looking across these lawns? It was here she did the first painting she ever sold. You can't help your heart aching for something like that.

When the sun lingered in the evening Albert would sometimes wait before hanging the thick curtain on its hooks at the kitchen window. On Wednesday of the third week, on a whim, he opened some wine, saying they would spin it out with the soup, make two days of it, if they went easy. There were only three bottles of soup left. But the Madiran and the melancholy autumn sunlight that evening made them forget and they finished the lot. Lucy watched him fetch the brandy from the dresser. There were fragments of some little sweet biscuits in the tin. Biscuits didn't keep for ever and she poured them out onto a plate. He grinned at her, sorting the broken bits into two piles with his finger, pushing them around. That was when the noise began. He could not hear it yet, but it was there: outside in the woods, dogs were barking.

No one kept a dog anymore. It had started shortly after the bread shop closed. People began letting dogs loose in the forest. Some must have found a way home, to be abandoned afresh. She often wondered what became of them. The poor things must have starved, most of them. But a few survived somehow. They passed their time barking at the moon or at passing strangers. Albert went to the window and peered across the lawn. There was no moon that night.

'If it's them coming, they're making a racket about it.'

It was the fault of the wine: she felt dizzy, but somebody should go and look at the other door. 'I suppose they'll come up the drive. You wouldn't know to come across the terrace. I'll go and look.'

'We don't know it's anybody yet. Just dogs gone mad. Perhaps one of them has made a kill. Stay where you are. I'll leave the blackout down, it won't hurt this once. They'll see the light for miles ... if there is a they, that is. I'll believe these visitors when I see them.'

The howling stopped eventually. Standing at the window, their shadows stretched out across the terrace, fingers of light falling on the edge of the grass. Beyond that, everything was black. The stonework of the pillars outside suddenly lit up. An arc of light, white and very bright, spun quickly across the terrace wall, blinding them as it struck the window and became black again. Something metal scraped against a wooden beam and clattered onto the stonework. There was a muttered curse and Albert chuckled. 'He's English anyway. That's a blessing. I've been meaning to hang that watering can up. It's been there for months.' He sounded excited, like a schoolboy. Someone tapped on the door then, without waiting, pressed the latch and slowly pushed it open. A face looked inside.

Perhaps it was the wine. She suddenly found herself a little girl standing in this exact place, pushing Laura forward to say something in French to Madame Berri. They had all been there, Elizabeth as well. And Stuart, trying to shush them all up. Curious - she had been standing just here. Perhaps it was wine inducing this strange fugue and it would pass. Because it was Stuart pushing the door open, not shushing her up at all, giving her a shy grin, the way you do when you feel embarrassed surprising someone.

'Hello Poppy, old girl. God, what's the matter? You're so thin. You look awful.'

'Not much to eat here.'

Had she spoken? Somebody had, certainly, but the exchange made no sense. It was surely the wine. Bad enough to be hallucinating, but somehow worse to find yourself talking to it, whatever it was. She had better sit down.

Albert had stepped back and was leaning against the window, patting his pocket for a cigar. 'God, Stuart of all people, you're a turn up. Sit down, Lucy, before you fall down, it's only the shock. I'll get him a drink.'

Stuart had been wearing a pair of incongruous wire-framed spectacles. He pulled them off with a grimace and looked round the room. 'Weird to be here - it seems like yesterday. Can't say how nice it is. Nothing's changed. You neither – I remember the way you always used to say Lucy.'

Albert was going to say something then glanced at her and stopped. As she folded her arms round Stuart, he draw in at her touch. She was so thin, that was the trouble; she knew it. And he was frightened of hurting her. There was a smell of damp tweed and leather about him. She felt like an insect clinging to a tree. You couldn't help crying, feeling like that. So she let him mumble things as she leaned her head back to get a better look at him, her face smeared with tears, crying and smiling, letting him mumble and grin back at her, running his hands through the hair at her neck.

A glass of brandy appeared perilously in Stuart's free hand. 'About the Lucy thing – that's a story for another time. A bit complicated. Have a drink if she'll let you. I thought there were two of you.'

'There are. We couldn't risk two bicycles down the hill so we tossed for who went first.' He detached himself and slumped into a chair, draining the brandy, his familiar voice still oddly out of place, looking up at her, pulling at her hand, shaking it.

'It is me you know, old girl. We were due ages ago, but this business is made of delays. Did you never think it might be?'

What could you say to that? If they could ask questions you could ask what business. But no, she had never given it any thought. They had not imagined anything. He simply didn't understand how little space there was here for imagining things.

'When this job came up I volunteered – you bet I volunteered. They might have said no of course - they always say no, that's normal. I told them we knew the place better than anybody - could even draw them maps. I think minds were changed. So there you are. I say, there wouldn't be another one of these would there? We've been dodging about since dawn.'

He had turned away and you could look. There was a subtle change about him, an indefinable nervous energy stretching the skin of his face, his whole body tense with a self absorption so complete he seemed barely present. He sat on the edge of the seat, one foot drumming out an urgent unconscious rhythm on the rug.

'How long will you stay?' As soon as she said it, she blushed at the idiocy of the question. Whatever next? Would they care to stay for lunch? Would they be coming to church? She saw the hint of a smile cross his face and rushed on, 'Sorry, I forgot – no questions. It's getting cold in here. I'll make you something hot. No milk I'm afraid. No coffee, come to that. We drink a sort of herb tisane – you get used to it. I'll put your brandy in it. The doctor said you'd be bringing food. I hope he's right. We've barely got any. You must remember the doctor? You spent long enough with him when we had our holidays here.'

'Food's on the way. It's late because that's where he's going.' Lucy was frowning at him, not following. 'I mean that's where he was making for first: the doctor's. If it's safe, of course. That's who I'm with. It's his uncle after all.'

The shock of his words lurched into her heart before she heard them properly. He had stopped speaking at the same time as the thudding began in her ears. He had seen the colour rise in her face and an unforgiveable silence fell on the room. He followed her glance to the clock and checked his watch, a small unthinking gesture to avoid her eyes. But he knew well enough;

they both knew. That was why he was here first, more like John the Baptist than tossing for anything. Checking she would be alright. Well, why wouldn't she be? The last thing she wanted was sympathy; not his, at any rate. Because she could feel sorry for herself whenever she felt like it. Which, when it came to Oscar, was quite often, damn it.

Stuart was looking down, pulling his feet back from the fire, embarrassed, casting round for something to say. Albert broke the silence but he must have seen by then she was not listening. He must have seen that, whether they cared or not, she was already far out into the night, waiting blindly between the dark trees, listening for the dogs. He must have been looking at her but she could only see woods. He must have been looking at her. Perhaps he could hear the words singing in her head. *Oscar is here.*

Albert had sacrificed another bottle of Pia's soup, quietly heating it at the stove, stirring, and pouring it into a bowl. As Stuart ate, he began to speak. Now Oscar was out, he was like a man freed from a vow of silence, unaware, as he talked, that eyes helplessly watched each movement of his spoon. He pushed the pan across the table, casually inviting them to take some. Albert carefully measured a little out, eating slowly. In the lamplight he looked almost himself again, somehow not so gaunt. As he finished, he lit a little cigar, leaning his chair back against the wall, blowing smoke into the air, watching Stuart's face as he talked.

Stuart's voice was there, floating past her, filling the quiet room. You could hear if you wanted, but she was barely listening. Stories of war: England's war. Mostly stories of destruction. He seemed almost to take satisfaction in listing familiar places consigned to the flames. It was like a hellish version of a children's game: Albert would mention a place and swing his chair forward to hear, "That's gone I think, some time ago now," or, "There's been a raid there, it's pretty grim, you can't get through, most of the street's gone." Or you would hear of someone they once knew well, "He's dead, I'm afraid," or,

"She's gone. Months ago. Caught it in a raid - all of them." It was not proper - he seemed to have forgotten how to speak of the dead. Saying all of them was wrong – a whole family needed more than that. Perhaps you simply stop mourning when there are too many – it was a shocking idea. They had mourned for Paul. She still mourned him and the thought of that misnamed grave made her weep. Perhaps you can only mourn one at a time.

'Is Mother alright?' She should say something. She should have asked before. Stuart's pitiless catalogue of horrors had somehow locked her brain. 'Father – where is he?' She barely recognised her own voice, 'And Laura? And Ian – what's he up to?'

'Father's ship was sunk in the raid on Portsmouth. It's alright - he was on leave. At home would you believe it? That's how luck goes. The doc says his heart's a bit dicky, should ease up a bit, but he's alright. Mother's not been too good. She's getting along. I tell her she should move out but you know what she's like. Laura's a WAAF. She joined up the week we declared war.' It was comforting to hear "we" like that: he didn't know yet about the New France. 'She does things with photographs ... no, forget that. I'm not supposed to know, so that must go for you as well. Laura's alright ... happy really. I got some leave just before this and she was fine. Ian was in uniform for a while. Army I think, but somebody told me he'd been taken on for something else. God knows what he's doing. It's a secret. We never see him.'

She had asked enough, done enough. She had to think of the woods. It was cold tonight, perhaps colder in the woods. She was going to see Oscar. She thought she would never see him again and he would be here, in this very room, tonight. And with the thought came a dizziness, a realisation the fire was making her eyes hurt, was making her light-headed. Stuart's voice was booming now, far away, hard to hear. He seemed not to notice he had an echo. How long did Albert say they would stay? It didn't matter; Oscar was what mattered. He'd be hungry when he got here. There was still soup in that pan. She would heat it up. If she heated the soup he would be bound to come. The syllogism wove itself round her brain until it seemed a good idea to stand up. To get up before the wave of sickness engulfing her made getting up impossible. She had not noticed before – there was a greasy taste to the soup. That sort of taste made you retch. It was certainly better to get up, to make for the door before the pain low down got too bad. It was bad already, sharp and bright making her sweat. Something heavy seemed to be dragging its way through her bowels. It was cooler in the dark of the corridor, clawing her way out, wondering whether she would be in time. As the door closed behind her she heard Albert's voice, 'It's alright. Leave her.' He sounded almost angry. 'Can't you see? She's starving. We've neither of us had any proper food for months. Leave her be.'

Pressing her forehead against the ice-cold of the bathroom mirror, willing away waves of nausea, she had not seen her face close like this for months. There were hundreds of tiny fissures across the surface of her skin, like crazed china. She pulled back and stared at herself, resting her hands on the basin. A corner of her mouth had cracked open, not bleeding, but red and raw. She had not noticed that before. There was a black edge to the hole. It should hurt, a thing like that, but it didn't. She put a finger to her face. It felt like the carapace of some dead insect. She would hardly be startled if it all detached and simply fell off like a dry shell. War had done this to her, endless months of barely eating had formed this gaunt skull. She had stopped noticing - had become comfortable with this bony caricature of a face. Two dark eyes stared back, unconcerned. This is why Stuart had looked away, hurt as if she had struck him. And when Oscar came? The dark eyes looked on, imperturbable, unconcerned. It was almost a surprise to see tears well up.

They had been talking about her when she came back into the room. You can always tell with that sort of silence. Now they were stumbling over each other to say something. Albert raised his hand and winked as she sat at the table. It was just enough to draw her into a smile. He pushed a glass towards her and started to pour, continuing even as she shook her head.

'You have to. This is by way of a toast. Here's a bit of news, Lucy. It's alright, he knows about Lucy. Here's a bit of welcome news. Stuart's gone and got himself married - can you believe it? That's worth a drink. Or two drinks when you know who to.'

'Of course I can believe it. It's Elizabeth isn't it? She as good as told me ages ago.' She smiled into Stuart's face, wincing at the sore on her lips. 'I knew she had you in her sights; that's the way these things are done. Lucky man – there's only one Elizabeth. I'd better not drink much. All this food – we're not used to it. Honestly, I wish you every happiness. You deserve it. Elizabeth as well. It's just right.' Albert was lighting another cigar; two in one night. 'That'll make him your real nephew now, won't it? I'm never any good at these family tree things.'

Stuart had suddenly got up, his back to the fire, trying to make himself look taller. When he looked like that, shy and awkward, pushing the hair out of his eyes, you had to think what funny things men were. And she almost wanted to kiss him.

'Lots of the chaps are getting married now. It's quite the thing. Awfully hard on Elizabeth, though. She'll be on her own a lot, but she said we'd better get on and do it, things being what they are.' It was speech with too many traps. Forcing them into embarrassed silence. He tried to pick up the thread, 'Of course, she's on her own now - God knows when this business will be over.'

But whether he meant the war or this mysterious visit she would never know. They were not to ask questions.

CHAPTER 11

Dreaming; then torn out of it by something huge and dreadful. Startled wide awake, heart pounding, blind in the silent dark. This dark was all wrong - the wind must have blown the shutters closed. It had been one of those awful dreams of falling that stop your heart; that was her first thought. You get those when you're hungry and she was always hungry now. But this seemed different. For one thing, whatever had woken her was still in the room, still there, roaring away in her head. No doubt about it: something huge had been in the room. Been and gone, disturbing the air, leaving its trace on the silence. The hell of it was, it had broken a dream of Oscar – and when did she dream of him? Almost never, damn it. The dream had started some other way. It was already fading, perhaps it was never clear how Oscar came into it, dreams were like that. But he was certainly there, deliciously insinuating himself into a sleep deeper than for months. Naked. And that had seemed perfectly as it should be, no cause for panic, just the soft calm of sleep, watching the two of them as he melted through the covers, his skin against hers, the touch of it like silk, soft watered silk. They were on *Malapet* – it must have been there – lying warm at the margin of the beach, shallow water creaming milky white against them, ribbed sand touching her flesh, the tide lifting effortlessly from below like irridescent silk. Floating; her head touching his hair. And watching the two of them it was certain in the logic of this dream she would give herself to him after an endless luxury of time. Under the immense *Malapet* sky filled with circling gulls. Gulls wheeling and calling. Gulls diving, calling, screaming. Until a monstrous ribbon of noise ripped through the dark, tipping the room, bursting over her, trailing away into a throbbing silence. And she was sitting hard up against the rough of a stiff French bolster, the pounding in her head like a hammer, staring sightlessly into thick black.

There were fumes in the room, faint but definite on the cold crisp of the air. It was hard to find the window, stumbling about in the dark, thinking of Albert lost in his graveyard. With the shutters back, a rush of rain hit her face. Rain, and the smell of petrol. Petrol everywhere. There were people down there, invisible thuds of running feet on grass, shadows rearing up against the woods. At the far edge of the lawn an astonishing sight: a vast fire burning itself out. A Wagnerian pyre, red embers swirling up in titanic clouds of smoke. They must have used petrol, too much petrol because the smell was everywhere. There was a dim figure darting in front, drawing back, throwing something. Then it was gone, leaving the cold night air filled with blustering smoke. Nothing but darkness and drumming rain.

She took particular care dressing that morning, unwilling to explain to herself exactly why. There was a frock, a treasured relic of London life: woollen stuff, long but just possible. It didn't look too bad. It had not had an outing for years. The wool smelled vaguely damp as she pulled it on. It made her seem fragile rather than skeletal, which was more than she could have hoped for in the circumstances. There was lipstick on the dressing table. How long since she had worn lipstick? But people do wear lipstick, red being better than blue when it comes to lips. Albert would see of course, but to hell with that, he wouldn't say anything. Albert was kind when he wanted to be. So lipstick it was, taking an age in the feeble light, the mirror gradually showing a kind of haggard clown staring at her. No. Not lipstick, after all. Oscar would just have to put up with her. Then she remembered Emily.

The huge front door had been left wide open, letting the smell of petrol into the house. White trails of smoke hung over the steps outside like steam, the yellow light from the hall cutting across slanting rain. That door had not been opened for months. It made the house seem vulnerable. There were sounds from the kitchen, the rattle of crockery, a murmur of men's voices. Albert must be making breakfast; that accounted for one of them. But the other? Quiet, slow, patient, always letting the other chap have his say. She knew it, of course: her heart got there first, hearts seem not to forget. So he was here at last, chattering for all the world as if nothing at all was amiss. He had come after they had given up waiting and all gone to bed. That was the sort of trick he played, he always liked the advantage, did Oscar. Well, she would see about that, lipstick or not

She pushed the door open and was disarmed at a stroke by the delicious scent of coffee. The warm room was full of it. They had not had coffee for months. Where on earth had it come from? They made an odd tableau, the two men, heads close together in the lamplight, lost in earnest conversation. You could paint it if you had a taste for pastiche Rembrandt: *Conspiring Gentlemen* - something like that. They had not heard her and sprang apart as she closed the door. Oscar turned, a smile lighting up his face, holding Albert's arm, muttering something. A single word. Not a whisper, but impossible to catch it all the same. They were up to something, these two, and whatever he said released a tension between them.

A tired looking man in a shabby black suit, shiny at the elbows was smiling at her. Was this her Oscar? He seemed dreadfully changed, the assurance gone, replaced by something almost furtive. She had not reckoned on his changing as well. He seemed not to look at her frock. It was her eyes he wanted, so best let him look there. Churlish to complain if a chap wanted to look at your eyes, and he did seem to want to do that very much. It was infuriating; she could not think how long it had been. Or where? Then the reason struck her and she let her eyes fall. He had been with her all the time. She lived with this man, the only oddity being he didn't know; it was embarrassing. Albert was forcing a cup of coffee into her hands, prising her fingers open. He had not looked so excited for months. 'Here. Grab this. Oscar brought it. God, I've missed coffee.' A curious glance thrown to Oscar, almost seeking permission about something; then, 'You needn't have got up, you know. It's early. We were hoping you'd get a bit of sleep. I suppose all the goings on outside got you up.'

Albert was talking but she barely heard him. She had been matching this changed Oscar against remembered encounters. Infuriating. If only she could think when last she had seen him. He seemed smaller. The Oscar in her dream had been lots taller than this man. No, perhaps that wasn't fair – they had been lying down, after all – and suddenly she was blushing like a girl. But you couldn't help noticing he seemed less tall – perhaps war did that to you, bent you to its will. His hair was the same, though: dark brown, curiously crinkly. No streaks of grey, that was a mercy. She was close enough to judge his skin. Perhaps not silk, but nice skin all the same. Easily the sort you might want to touch. Now she came to think about it, that dream had been a help, completing the preliminaries, as it were. You could say they were ready to take up where things had been left off.

Although, shamefully, where exactly things had been left off was a mystery. Where had they met last? For God's sake, it was on the edge of her mind, somehow impossibly connected with cooking. Where on earth was it? He was standing, one hand stretched out to her, puzzled by her silence. Or puzzled by her blush; who knows? She had had a thought this morning, working with the lipstick, that he might greet her brushing her cheek, almost a kiss. The French do that, and he was as good as French. But she gave him her hand and he held it. That was alright as well: people shook hands in France, and if Albert had not grinned like that they could have stayed with linked hands for who knows how long. As she gently freed herself, he resisted for a second, smiling into her face, 'It was Saint-Valery - you surely remember?' That was Oscar all over. Always getting there first, somehow inhabiting her thoughts.

'Of course I remember. I remember you telling me to get away. I remember that. And it looks like I did the exact opposite. I'll tell you why later - it's a long story.'

He was staring inexplicably at Albert, frowning a little, hurrying on, talking over her, 'I hear you were all waiting up for me last night. Put it down to complications, you know ...' No doubt about it - he was changing the subject. For some reason he didn't want to talk about that night in Saint-Valery. Emily's night. The night she had been so late for that show – and that had been his fault as well. Hadn't he said he'd be shot if he said something or other? Whatever was that all about? Perhaps he'd said whatever it was, by accident. All she could remember was his talking about Emily. There had been enough Emily that night to be shot for.

He was trying to catch her eye, 'Things to do, you see. You'll never guess how I got here. I couldn't risk the road. Stuart took that route and we always go separate ways, that's a rule. You never know who might decide that two bicycles in one day looks fishy. The trouble with France now is people think everything is fishy. Everybody putting in reports all the time. Uncle's place is full of them, denunciations mostly, piles of them. I came pushing the bike through the woods, plus a jerry can of petrol. Not easy with just a torch, I can tell you – it took for ever. And I suppose you know the place is full of dogs – I wasn't expecting dogs. I didn't see them, but they're everywhere. Kicking up an awful racket just when you don't want it.'

In happier times she could listen to this quiet voice for ever. But he was gabbling; talking for the sake of it. Steering her away from something. It was like listening to one of those elaborate lies on the wireless, impressively filled with circumstantial truth. Don't conjurors do that? Make you look at one hand while the other is about its business. God knows why, but he was doing that - trying to put her at ease about something. It was the wrong way round - he was the visitor here. He tapped her arm, 'You're miles away. I said I've brought peace offerings: coffee, sugar, eggs – four of them, miraculously unbroken.'

Albert held an egg up to the light. 'You don't know what this means to us. It must be a year since we've seen an egg. I'm going to save the shells for a still life.' Maybe everything was askew this morning because she had been startled out of her sleep, but Albert seemed to be playing the same game. Talking nonsense. Why this sudden heartiness? What was there to be hearty about? It was wrong, wrong, wrong. Albert read something in her face and was suddenly serious, the grin vanishing, 'Look, I'll make us all some breakfast as soon as Stuart gets back. Did you hear the aeroplane?'

He had seen she was annoyed. Where was Stuart? Gets back from where? Why was everything being only half-said all of a sudden? How could she not have heard that enormous noise? Why did nobody mention the petrol smell everywhere? Did they think she'd not notice the whole house reeked of it? Did they think she'd somehow not notice a huge bonfire? This was about more than finding a room for couple of blokes. Come to think of it, Albert had taken his time telling that story; what else was he holding back? You couldn't help feeling angry, locked out like this. Locked out by an insufferable conspiracy of men. The worst was realising so late that it had all been planned – all of it. And she had been intended not to know. It was unbearable.

'I heard the awful noise in my room, if that's what you mean. I didn't know it was an aeroplane. How could I? It had gone before I could know. All I remember was the noise. It woke me up. I'd been dreaming.' Why on earth had she mentioned the dream? What had that got to do with it? Just when the little speech had been going so well - suitably cold, leading to a haughty protest. Oscar had seen she was angry. Trust her to go and spoil everything, stupidly looking at him just when she thought of that dream. It wasn't fair, being undone by your own thoughts – or was it more than thoughts? And as she idiotically wondered whether he knew about dreams as well, she felt her face flush.

But Oscar had turned away, already speaking to Albert: 'They use a Whitley for drops ...' She knew exactly what he was doing, brisk phrases cutting her out. Things not to worry her with. Things she would never know about. All the same, that was not why he had turned away. He had seen something in her eyes, only for a fraction of a second, but in that moment he had seen to her core. She felt suddenly naked.

The talk now was for Albert, men's stuff: bombers; night flying; low runs. 'The Whitley's got the range and some to spare, that's the point. What makes this place ideal is you come in over the sea. The Whitley's alright, a nice enough crate, I've not flown them, but Stuart has. Doesn't stand much of a chance if they put fighters up but you're alright this far South. Just keep out of harm's way – that's the name of the game. In and out before they know you've been. Like last night - the noise will have woken the place up, that's for sure, but she's right - it's all over before you can say snap. I'll warrant nobody will have seen that fire. Even if they did, Stuart's covered it by now.'

Suddenly she was "she". They had forgotten about her, not even looking at her. But at least Stuart was still here, somewhere. The aeroplane had dropped something and he had been out there waiting for it. It sounded impossible in the dark, but there must be ways of doing these things, parachutes, something like that - men's tricks: things she wouldn't know about. Oscar suddenly broke off with an unconvincing laugh, pushing one of the gift eggs towards her hand in a placatory gesture, 'You know, I remember you with that fierce look. I bet you don't, but I'll never forget it. It's alright, you know - with luck, nobody will have seen a thing, honestly.'

'I hadn't realised you had to be lucky. I'm not a very lucky person. Painters aren't lucky. I'm telling you that now, so you know. And it's only fair to ask about things we never expected. We didn't know about the aeroplane. Ask Albert here, we didn't know anything about it, or a fire, come to that.' Albert was peering guiltily into his cup, stirring a sugar lump he didn't need, picking flecks of paint off the heel of his thumb. His whole repertoire of gestures; she knew them all. He knew all about it. Albert couldn't tell lies for toffee. 'What do we do if the police come asking? You don't know what it's like here. The police are French, there's no Germans here, but it's worse. They've changed. We're in hiding as much as you are, don't you realise that? And I've only got my shop ticket to show who I am. That and a dodgy old rail pass – it's pathetic. It only works because nobody cares, don't you see? I'm scared all the time. I have to get away with this Lucy business and if people come asking I won't be able to. My French isn't up to it.'

Oscar had heard the desperation in her voice and exchanged a look with Albert, for a moment lost for words. He took her hands and held on as she pulled away, steadying her, looking at her eyes, 'I'm sorry. It'll work out. Just wait a bit, let things settle. They only decided on the drop at the last minute. Before that, we were bringing the stuff by train. But trains are no-go now, even with the best paperwork ...' He had stopped, looking like a man who had already said too much, already given something away, although it was impossible to know exactly what. 'Seriously, there won't be a trace. The fire's gone. You wouldn't find that spot now, even if you looked. And we're not here, remember? Unless they come with twenty men and surround the place.'

'Who's "they"? Nobody comes here. We haven't seen anybody for months. And what did your aeroplane drop - can we know that?'

Again that irritating glance at Albert; again a hesitation, 'What you don't know, you can't tell. That's why no questions comes into it. You'll never see it, I promise you. That's Stuart's job and he's good at it.'

'Glad to hear I'm valued.' Stuart's voice had broken a long silence, Lucy fuming in her chair. He had been standing in the doorway behind them, perhaps for some time, listening. He held a short tube made of ribbed metal awkwardly under one arm. His face was smeared with wood smoke and he was soaked through, but the tension in his face had gone, he seemed almost cheerful. He was looking hard at Oscar, suddenly serious, 'This is the little one we need. And the others are safe.' He slumped into a chair, resting the tube across his knees, 'I say, any hope of breakfast? And before you say no, I have a little magic to perform.' He began releasing leather catches along the side of the tube, spilling a curious hot metallic smell into the room, a memory of where the thing had been. It split open like a clamshell. Half was jammed full of anonymous steel tins each with a white gummed label. On the other side, barely visible behind thick green webbing, rows of oilskin parcels jammed together. 'Now ... more coffee?' He had ripped the webbing off and was juggling with little waxed parcels. 'Or perhaps chocolate? Mind you, let me tell you, standard issue cocoa leaves a lot to be desired. No ... what we want is this.' He had broken open a huge packet, enough for weeks. The scent of ground coffee was everywhere.

Oscar tapped Stuart's shoulder, a tiny gesture, calling him back, 'Manage alright?'

'Not a hitch. Came over dead centre and pulled away like a lift. Glad it wasn't me, you lose your breakfast that way. But the drop couldn't have been better. You could hear things breaking for yards,' grinning at Lucy, patting the back of her hand, 'Don't worry, sister dear, just branches.' He pulled a folded map out of his pocket, dropping it onto the table in front of Oscar.

'The cache. Marked as close as I can get it. Mind you, I'm pleased with myself – they'll have a hell of a job finding it.'

Breakfast turned into an indeterminate disorganised feast and there was no point pretending she was part of it. They were like schoolboys clustered round a new toy. Something unwelcome had come into the house along with the metal tube. Hard to put a name to it - a disturbing sense of nervous energy, felt more in her stomach than her head. That feeling you had forgotten something vitally important and would pay for the forgetting. They were all waiting for something undefined to happen. Life had been bad enough when they were starving; well fed, it seemed worse. She slipped unnoticed out of the kitchen, feeling slightly sick, and climbed the stairs to the studio.

It was not so very long before she heard Albert's tap on the door. You couldn't help smiling, because he only ever knocked when there was a quarrel to make up. He pushed the door wider and peered in. 'I thought you'd be here. I've brought you some coffee, and I didn't think I'd say that again. I've been thinking about Paul's painting. I've an idea what to do with it.'

'You mean hide it before the police get here? I imagine they'll have more on their mind than looking for paintings.' But she went on smiling all the same, just to take the taste away.

'Honestly Lucy, nobody's looking for anybody. They know what they're doing, those two. Look, do you want me to say sorry? I didn't know about all this song and dance, and that's the truth. J-P didn't tell me much about it. Just nods and hints. I don't think the poor chap knew much himself – they wouldn't tell him.' He was casting about for the right thing to say. 'I thought we just had to hide a couple of spies, I suppose that's the word, sounds bloody silly to me. I had no idea it was going to turn personal. I'll bet anything neither did J-P. They wouldn't risk telling him that. If you want me to, I'll say I'm sorry I got us into this. I was just so worked up about Paul. I should have told you I expected that plane – J-P said it was possible. He kept saying the fewer people knew, the better. One thing, though. You've seen Stuart, and you've seen your precious Oscar again – you can't have expected that. And we've got food for a good while. Oscar called it a special delivery, by the way, a sort of thank-you.'

'He's not my precious Oscar. And it's a bit rich saying thanks when I never knew what they were up to. And I still don't. I'm not stupid, Albert, they're not doing all this to bring us coffee and biscuits. What's it about? What did the aeroplane drop?' She could ask him. The rule about questions didn't apply between them. And Albert surely knew; why had he been so shifty? Why else all those irritating secret glances? Surely she had a right to know, given she might die for knowing it.

'I think Oscar's hoping I'll do the explaining. It's all a bit weird. Not what I expected. Let's settle Paul's painting first, then we can talk.'

She fetched the painting from behind the stack of canvases and laid it on the table for him. It was not the sort of thing to look at in daylight. True, once you started looking you found it hard to stop, but not because of anything you would want to see. Certainly not that. She remembered once seeing a cat hit by a passing car. What was left of it could not live, but refused to die, so its being alive, writhing itself into a pool of blood, became your own particular torment. A torment worse than the cat's. That was when you prayed for death. Paul's painting lay there and you dared not look away, even when tears started to your eyes. Suddenly the squabble with Albert seemed childish. She stretched out and took his leathery hand. 'What was it Elizabeth used to say? *Pax*, was that it? Well, *Pax*. Let's sort out what we do with this. The other things don't matter.'

He started rummaging among canvases stacked against the wall, crouching down, working his way along. Finally, he found what he had hidden and pulled it out. 'Good job Paul took one of my stretchers - it's the same. Help me get the frame off this.

'But it's *Girl with Straw Hat* – you're not going to do anything with that? You can't!'

'Nothing drastic. You'll see.' He briefly checked the frame against Paul's canvas then left it lying there. 'Just hold her while I get the wedges out. I'm going to get it off its stretcher. It's alright, I used to know how to do this.'

As he prised out the tacks, the solemn face of the girl in the old-fashioned hat distorted and grew limp. It was clear what he intended and long before he finished, she was raking through the table drawers for tacks. He gently fitted the stiff fold of painted canvas over Paul's and tacked it in place. There was a pot of glue on the floor. He lit the little stove under it, waiting while the place filled with the stench of burnt flesh, stirring white pigment into the pot, finally running a loaded brush along the seam at the back. 'Old Vuillard taught me this trick. He painted with this stuff - still does for all I know. I couldn't see the point, it dries like smoke; doesn't leave you time for second thoughts. He said that was the point, so I told him I like second thoughts. It's just the ticket for this, though.' He was already tapping wedges in, pushing the double canvas into its frame, holding it up. A sad girl with pale blue eyes and a straw hat gazed limpidly into the space beyond them.

'What do you think? Paul always liked this painting you know. Kept telling me to show it. He liked the girl, to tell you the truth. But he knew she was mine, so we didn't fight over her. To think, she was dead a year after I did this. Influenza. Took her in five days. I thought I'd never get over it. After she died I must have painted her twenty times. In the end I simply didn't believe she'd gone. Still don't. That's when I learned what frauds painters are.'

'I don't see it makes you a fraud.'

'Oh yes you do. It's being outside things all the time. You get so you can't feel things right. Don't go telling me you don't know that.'

He was right, of course. That was why Paul's painting was so cruel. Not something you looked at, but something that did your looking for you. And who would like what they saw then?

It was unlike him, but Albert was tidying things up, fussing, taking the pot off the stove, pouring tacks back into the box, clearing the table, gazing about, wondering where things went. As he stooped to slide the painting back among the others he looked up at her, 'I was a disappointment to him, you know. He knew I could see what he was up to and he thought we'd do things together. Wanted me to come with him. Tried to push me that way. But I didn't want to go where he was going, I'm not sure he ever understood that. I think that's why he was so excited finding you. The funny thing is, he wouldn't understand your stuff now. Still, he always liked a joke.'

She never saw Paul's painting again. No one did.

CHAPTER 12

For some time there had been sounds from the floor below: a low murmur of voices, unaccustomed feet creaking on the stairs up to the corridor. They felt as if they were listening for burglars. Albert seemed to feel whispering was appropriate: 'I'll bet you that's Stuart sorting his room out. He said they shouldn't be sleeping in the house because they need a clear line of escape. I thought he was joking. It sounds mad. I told him they were welcome to sleep in my studio across the terrace, there's a bed in there. The fire smokes, but they can put up with that. Or there's the day bed in the Garden Room. The room's damp, but it's on the ground floor and he can jump out of the window if he feels like it. If he can get the thing to open, I never can. Does all this sound mad to you? I can't believe I got us mixed up in it. It doesn't feel real somehow.'

But Albert was certainly wrong. The more these little domestic things pressed in on her, the more real it all seemed. They had somehow crossed into unknown territory and it was too late to go back now. It was why she felt sick all the time. It was all too late. Too late to ask exactly what they had wished on themselves. At the back of her mind was the word "spy", a childish word she could hardly articulate for the shame of it. How could Stuart be a spy?

Listening to the elaborately discreet sounds below had been a barricade against thought. The sudden silence downstairs meant the dam broke. A clear line of escape; what on earth did Stuart mean? The sweep of lawn to the distant trees seemed dreadfully exposed. What if those policemen came back? What if they arrived right now? It took seconds for a car to appear. Don't they shoot spies? And those harbouring spies? Or was that just Jews? Why Jews anyway? She could not help thinking of Oscar and Stuart out there, hopelessly vulnerable, darting over the open grass. It was too far; you can't outrun a bullet. Standing immobile at the window, blindly staring at the unreachable trees, she realised her whole life had been lived unused to fear. Unused to the feel of it on her skin.

Albert was wiping glue off his fingers, snagging a bit of rag between his fingers, managing a crooked sort of grin, trying to read her face. 'God, you look tragic. We'll get it sorted out, you know. I was only joking. They can sleep where they like. We're safe enough. Look, why don't you talk to Oscar? Get it all from the horse's mouth. He's the one in charge, he told me that. He was going to explain what they were up to when you came in just then. The poor chap clammed up. I'll tell you this, he's scared of you ... no, don't shake your head, I know what I'm saying. The pair of you circling round each other like two panthers in a cage. It's been that way since you were a kid. If you want him, why don't you put him out of his misery? You owe it yourself: there's only one life to live.'

'I don't know what you mean. Anyway, you know well enough he's not mine for the taking. Didn't you know that?'

'Have it your own way. Just remember I'm not all that old. Not dead yet, anyway. I remember feeling that way myself.'

Dear old Albert trying his best; pretending not to fight with Paul over the woman he loved. The woman they both lost. Albert remembering his girl in the straw hat, the one who died. And he didn't know she had lost as well, ages ago, in Saint-Valery.

'Albert, can't you see we can't keep two grown men here out of sight if somebody really comes looking? Perhaps a day or two, but not more. The whole idea was stupid. Yes, it's lovely to see Stuart – oh, and Oscar as well, if that pleases you. But I'll be in a funk till they go and that's the truth. Did they say how long? Did Oscar tell you why they're here?'

'I hate to harp on the fact, it really must be love. The question isn't why they're here, it's why *they* are here? Haven't you wondered? Do you believe in coincidences? Because I don't, not two at a time.'

Suddenly she realised it was true; she had given no thought to it at all. Of all the airmen in the world, her own brother on the doorstep. Then Oscar. Albert was right, coincidences like that don't happen. The truth was, since Oscar had arrived, it had been enough just to be close to him. Like a lovesick schoolgirl she had settled for that. "If you want him," Albert had said – God, if that was all it took.

He was fiddling with the box palette fixed to the end of the table, scraping off dabs of colour with his nail. He looked up at her, a hard look, his gravelly voice just a rumble. 'I should have explained. You see why they sent Stuart, don't you? It's because of you. I was thinking they were here because of you – to get you away from here. But I got the wrong end of the stick: they want us both away – he as good as admitted it when he got me on my own this morning. This is all some mad scheme to get us both away.' It was a bleak look, fierce eyes telling her he would not be going. He would not be abandoning the Pink House, not even if he died here. He gave a brief shrug, making for the door, shaking the idea away, 'I'll dig Stuart out. Sort out somewhere for him to sleep. You see what you can get out of young Oscar. Go easy on him.'

Before she reached the kitchen door she had already decided Oscar would be sitting in the hard pine chair by the window that he had claimed for his own. Watching him there this morning he had seemed so absorbed in himself you could believe he saw nothing beyond the glass. He had known she was looking at him but didn't seem to mind, even took pleasure in it. He would be sitting there now, waiting for her. Perhaps Albert had said something to him. Perhaps he meant to account for himself. Perhaps he meant to account for Emily. That was more like it. She deserved that.

But when she opened the door, it was to walk into a room full of hushed voices, Oscar talking to someone in rapid French against the rush of another voice. Seeing her come in, a young man sprang up from the table, stumbling back, fixing her face with a terrified stare. He was little more than a boy dressed in nondescript peasant black. Although this was no peasant, there was intelligence in those frightened schoolboy eyes. The map Stuart had brought lay open on the table between them. Oscar scooped it up, crumpling it into his pocket.

She pushed the door to behind her. 'Sorry. I didn't know you had a visitor. And it's quite alright, I didn't come to pounce on your secrets.'

The reproach earned her a gentle apologetic smile but Oscar offered no explanation for the intruder. He seemed changed from this morning: still dreadfully tired, with black smudges under his eyes, but something new, a kind of restless urgency.

He let the map drop back onto the table. 'Sorry, second nature. Here, look if you like. It's where Stuart put the stuff from the drop. He marked the place.' He was waving towards the ribbed contraption on the table with its leather straps hanging loose. 'Five more like that, but bigger. Don't worry, they're well out of the way.'

'Only not food, I suppose?'

A long silence, head bowed, staring at his shoes, the boy throwing uncomprehending glances from one to the other, puzzled by the language. Incredibly, he was not going to answer. He was going to hang on to his secret and suddenly she was furious with him. How dare they invade the house like this, filling it with their secrets? And now strangers creeping about. Did they not realise the risk? It was intolerable. Perhaps he would never answer. In which case, she had nothing more to say to him. As if he realised, he raised his eyes to hers, almost painfully.

'No, not food.'

He stood up and put his arm on the boy's shoulder in an odd gesture, half dismissal, half affection, steering him to the kitchen door, holding it open until the last of his scampering feet across the terrace faded to nothing. When he turned and smiled into her eyes it was so unexpected her anger drained away. With the boy gone she could feel his relief.

'Always anticipate the unexpected, that's what they tell you in training. I think it's meant as a joke. Best we don't know who that little chap was. He kept trying to tell me his name until I told him to shut up. They were here last night, a couple of them; just schoolkids. They were in the woods, up to no good, setting snares I imagine, and saw the fire. It must have seemed quite an adventure. Stuart told them never to come back on any account. But the boy thought this news too important to keep to himself. Bad news I'm afraid, although it'll mean more to you than me.'

He had seemed so calm and that smile had turned her heart over. And now this – surely he knew there was only one sort of bad news. She saw two men running for their lives, desperate, hopeless, betrayed by their line of escape. Too far to run. Two men pitching forward one against the other, slaughtered beasts, shots bringing them down. She found herself gripping the back of the chair, fighting dizziness.

'Look you'd better sit down. It's not nice, but it's not what you think. No danger ... no immediate danger. The lad came with a story about the priest in the village, something he thought I should know. This priest - do you know him?'

'No, barely at all. Albert does; calls him the Abbé Constatin. A nice old chap. Goes round smiling at people for no good reason. Not Albert, though - he disapproves of Albert. Something to do with his rakish past I suppose. Why? What's he done now?'

'The police arrested him a couple of days back.'

'We know. They keep doing it. It's because he won't sign some paper. He says he can't because he's a priest. It's not all that serious. They always let him go.'

'It is serious. Apparently he had somebody hidden in the cellar in his house. He'd locked him in and told him to keep quiet while he went to fetch things from the church. That was when he got himself arrested again. After two days the man in the cellar was desperate and started banging on the door. It was just bad luck – it's always bad luck – the only people to hear him were a couple of policemen. They broke the door down.'

She already knew she didn't want to hear the end of this story. She had seen it in Oscar's face; he would not be telling it otherwise. Stories like this never ended well, she knew that much. She wanted to stop her ears like a child, tell him she knew the end, he needn't go on, but there was nothing in the kitchen but his quiet voice. She must hear it out, whatever the horror.

'He was Belgian. Jewish. Half starved anyway, because they had been sharing what bits of food they'd got. They brought the priest back and started questioning the two of them. The chap in the cellar was incoherent, out of his mind with thirst. He made a run for it. It was a bedlam. Policemen firing off pistols inside the house. They'd probably never used them before. One of them chased after and let off a shot in the street outside. Nine times out of ten you wouldn't hit a barn door with one of those things, they're more for show than anything else. The Belgian chap, it seems he'd got as far as the corner. He was unlucky. Got a bullet in his foot. He fell and the two of them were all over him. A bit crazy I suppose, that's how these things go. They shot him dead. And your priest as well.'

'NO!'

She had not meant to shout. Dreadful as it was to admit it, she had long before stopped listening, stopped thinking of the old priest. This was how it would be with Oscar; with both of them. They would be killed like that, in the same banal confusion, the two of them running across a lawn, making for woods they could never reach. She found herself staring at his face, at the set line of his lips, and was suddenly certain she could not bear it if her Oscar died.

'But why poor old Abbé Constatin? He couldn't run anywhere. He could barely walk. Why such a thing? Why?'

'I think it was their idea of summary justice. They're incredibly worked up about Jews. They really do believe that Jews caused all this misery. That boy saw it happen. He says one of them shot the priest in the head quite deliberately. He was sick on the way here, all over his best suit. Things just got out of hand - that's what happens. The police aren't soldiers. God knows why they're running about with pistols.'

He fell back into his chair looking up at her face, letting his eyes fall as he misunderstood the tears on her cheeks, the fact she could not stop her lips trembling. He seemed to be speaking to himself, '… but they would have seen him run away. Wondered where he was off to. Damn the boy, he shouldn't have come here. Curse it for bad luck.'

He was slumped down, barely alive. An unpleasant pose to draw, a mix of lethargy and extreme tension. She wanted to straighten him up, press his shoulders back, make him look at her again, make him smile in her eyes again, explain how for a reckless moment she had thought he was hers. Explain to him how terror had let that thought back into her mind.

It seemed an age before he spoke. He seemed to be answering a question in her face. 'I met up with Stuart about a year ago. He was flying out of … God no, I'd better not say where ... it doesn't matter where he was, he's not there now. Technically, I'm in charge of this show. No good reason. I'm older I suppose, and had a promotion on the cards. Three months ago we were both called to a meeting. Separately, not at the same time. You've seen the man, he was with me at Saint-Valery. He invited me to volunteer to join a Special Forces unit. Said the same to Stuart. I'm afraid that's how things are done. He said they were recruiting people with good French to form small commando groups operating in and out of France.'

'He couldn't have said that to Stuart. He can't speak French. He can barely get by. You've heard him.'

'I didn't find out about that until later. Look, how much do you know about the situation in France?'

'We live here. Does that count? Sorry, that's rude. But I could ask you the same question: how much do you know? Alright, you have your war - we call it your war - but there's no war here. All we have is people throwing their weight around. You surely didn't think country villages were full of nice kindly people helping each other? I suppose you do look out for people you really love, but I'm not sure even that's true anymore. I catch myself watching Albert cut the bit of meat, checking he's not cheating me. It's shameful. Our war is village toughs settling scores, eyeing you up, leering at you, pawing you if they get the chance. People you wouldn't have trusted with sixpence a while ago standing outside the grocers with pistols in their belts, pushing you in the back. Everybody spying on everybody else. All because there's nothing left, pretty well no food at all. So that's what I call the situation in France. Stuart told us about the fires in London, the bombing, the gas masks, and all that. It sounds like hell on earth. Our hell is nothing at all. We've stopped. We're starving. If we catch a cold … something like that … we'll just die. Is that what you wanted to know?'

She realised she was shouting, feeling sick, fighting back the humiliation of tears. No, she didn't want him to look at her - didn't want his pity. He could keep it for somebody else.

He put a hand out and let it rest on her arm. She felt the warmth of it and looked away blinking at tears, pressing his hand with her own, holding him there. He waited until she turned to him, tipping her face up to his own, 'I'm not crying ... I never cry. It's just you get out of the way of talking about things. You can't help getting worked up.'

'My fault. It was thoughtless. That boy coming. I didn't expect it. It's changed things. I was hoping we could stay a bit. Hoping we'd have time to talk. But it's too big a risk now. Damn that child.'

'We listened to the wireless a lot at first, about what you call the situation. About helping the war effort. The French war effort that is - ours, not yours. That was just after the armistice. I don't know whether we were expected to believe it. They went on and on about helping with the final push into England. They said England had lost, been invaded. I don't know about Albert, but I believed every word of it. It's stupid, but you believe the wireless, don't you? I thought it was true for ages and all I could think of was Mother and Laura.'

It was nice feeling his hand on her arm. If she stayed quite still perhaps he would not move; there was no reason for him to move. She managed a smile, 'I even spared you a thought or two. But no … there's no war here. Not a real war. No fighting. Just French policemen and thugs with guns in their belts. I know the invasion didn't happen, we worked that out when they stopped talking about it. But nobody was cheering here. France is full of Germans - how do we ever get them out? That's all people are asking. After what happened to those ships in Algeria, there's talk of England bombing Paris. If you win your war, what happens to us?'

'You remember Saint-Valery? When I told you to get out quick.'

'I remember a lot about Saint-Valery. I remember you made me dreadfully late. Actually, what I remember most is you saying you'd be shot for telling me something.'

'A bit dramatic. But, believe me, you wouldn't have wanted to be stuck in that place. It barely exists now.'

'I still came back here eventually. England didn't seem like home anymore, I think that was the reason. And then France lost, whatever that means. Just gave up, in spite of all those millions of invincible men. Nobody really understands it. The new lot seem to be running the place for the Germans. It's a strange setup, but you can't call it war. Nothing's happened here except Madame Berri ran away - and an old painter died of fear or anger or misery, or God knows what. More likely he died because he didn't want to take our food. So he let himself die and we can't forgive ourselves, although we had nothing to eat either. You wouldn't believe how fast it happens when you've nothing to eat. And we couldn't even bury him because he was Jewish – have you ever heard anything so … anything so … vindictive? Why?'

She could see the line of his hair where it had been cropped to brand him as a fighting man. There was a tiny scar high up on one cheek. It was very old. He must have got it as a child. His face was close to hers, his eyes fixing hers.

'This time I'm not being dramatic: I could be shot for telling you this.'

'Perhaps you shouldn't then.'

'Until that kid came barging in I wasn't going to. That's what comes of having no imagination. The people who plan these things never imagine an old priest locking somebody in his cellar. I wasn't going to tell you because I was ordered not to. Myself, I can't see why you shouldn't know, but it's not for me to decide. So I'm disobeying an order. You said nothing happens here … something like that. Well, that's going to change. Just don't ask me how I know. This is not going to be an abandoned bit of the unoccupied zone for much longer. In a matter of days - a couple of weeks at most - your French police will be playing second fiddle to German troops, fighting troops, thousands of them, all over the place. With the war in Africa now, they have to move South and to hell with your armistice. More to the point, we're pretty sure they will be right here. Even in this house. That's it. That's what I was ordered not to tell you. It's why we're here.'

'That's absurd! Why on earth the Pink House? I see now. Albert was right. I know what you're up to. You're trying to make us leave.'

He was looking at her, surprised. 'Make you? Surely, you want to? Look, sooner or later there's opposition to occupying forces, there always is. And there will be this time, armistice or not. In fact it's starting already. Our job – my job if you like - is to make sure of the *direction* of that opposition, do you understand what I'm saying? For God's sake, do you want to end up fighting England? Because that's what it may come to.'

'It's what Albert said. It's why we stopped listening to the wireless. He said they made even the truth sound like a lie.'

'You know I'm telling you the truth.' He had flushed with anger as she pulled her hand away. He was trembling, fumbling at an inside pocket, pulling out a flimsy scrap of yellow paper. 'Here – read it if you like. I shouldn't have kept it. You can die for keepsakes in my business. I was told to burn it.'

It had been torn off something longer and was virtually blank, just two lines of irregular characters. It must have been the end of the ribbon because the typist had stamped the keys, biting faint letters hard into the paper. Albert's name and her own were underlined in single dashes in red. There was something amateurish about it. If a thing was to have authority you expected more. It read, "*Also known to be in France. Repatriation a priority.*" It was initialled, no more than a scrawl, with a laconic addition in neat script at the foot, "*Arthur, see what you can do about this business.*" The ink was still bright; it could have been done yesterday.

Oscar waited until she handed it back. 'I got it the day before the drop. Until then they hadn't told us what it was really about. And before you ask, I had no idea Stuart was going to be involved. Obviously, they wanted him, once they knew who he was. It looks like I'm fated to turn up telling you to go home.'

'What about Albert? You'll never get him to leave. He'll say why should he? He's French – didn't you know that? This is his home. All his work is here. He'll never go.'

'Yes we knew about the nationality.'

'I do wish you'd stop saying "we", it makes you sound like a committee.'

'Just try to imagine this place full of Germans. You won't have seen the Paris newspapers? Not much starvation there, I can tell you. Not much war either. Streets full of tourists. In German uniform. Shops open, most of them. Music halls full. Life goes on. That was the deal: collaborate in the war effort and we'll let you get on with life. I suppose that goes for painters. Just get on with what you do and don't ask questions. So long as you're French. Not Jewish, of course. It's a different matter if you're Jewish.'

'Albert's French. I mean he's not Jewish. God, I don't know what I mean. Why shouldn't he be Jewish? Not that he is ...'

Oscar had stood up, looking into the fire, kicking a log, letting it fall in a shower of sparks. He seemed to know everything. Did he know about Paul? He was looking down at the top of her head. The way he had looked in Saint-Valery, buried in his uniform, a little lost.

'Think about it: two of England's most famous painters living and working in France. While people back home are burnt alive. Gassed. Can't you see?'

'That's not fair! We're starving. Look at me for heaven's sake! Do you think I've the strength to work? I can barely climb the stairs. Anyway, why shouldn't I work? Damn your war.'

He looked startled. 'I should have said I was the wrong person. Stuart as well, whether you're his sister or not. I should have explained there were personal reasons. They would have seen the point. I'd have made them.'

'I can't see I deserve all this fuss anyway. Yes, Albert's famous. Very famous in France. He can't help that. And you can say me as well, I suppose. But this war has nothing to do with it. And we're not that famous, you know. Not in the big scheme of things. The competition's quite severe.'

'All I have is that list. They want you out. We're to see to it. Albert as well, if he agrees.'

'What if I don't agree? Nobody knows I'm me, you know. I'm not the name on that paper – not here. I'm Lucile Beyrou here. Your uncle helped with the papers. Did you know that? If I keep my head down ...'

He was slowly shaking his head, smiling. Not altogether a nice smile, watching her stammer herself to a halt. 'The French know all about Lucy. I told Albert this morning - they've known for months. Pretty well right from the start. You're in their sights.

I keep telling you, don't believe what you're told. The fact of the matter is, not long from now you'll have German officers billeted here. Probably a nice enough chap. An art collector maybe, that's normally the sort who wangle this sort of posting. They're already collecting art work, didn't you know? Getting it donated you might say, because lots of artists are Jewish. Do I have to spell all this out? Your *Oberst*, or *SS-Standartenführer*, or whatever, will arrive complete with staff – even kitchen staff - and leave the two of you to get on with your painting. I imagine an ancient chap, not quite pensioned off, capable of keeping records and barking orders down the telephone. But plenty of scope for delicate after dinner discussions of art if that's what you want.'

He had talked himself out and fell silent, moodily staring through the window across to the woods. This bitterness had little to do with her, that was clear enough. It had been that boy coming back in all innocence, simply because he knew the way. Oscar was calculating, revising, thinking how best to short-circuit arguments. He had been hoping they could stay, that's what he said. The thought filled her with irrational pleasure.

He was trying again, 'Albert's French, I appreciate that's an issue. But you won't get people at home – I mean England – to understand all that stuff about armistice. All they know is France had an army of millions and decided to lie down and play dead. All they see is a whole people collaborating with the enemy. Alright, our enemy, not yours, but it's not a distinction anybody understands. In England we have nightmares about German troops in the street. People don't imagine collaboration, don't even think about it – it's too late. We're going to fight, don't you understand that? Probably lose. Certainly lose. It depends on the Americans ... how far they'll go. At the moment, we're losing ... going down fighting ...' He had run out of things to say and stood there waiting for her to speak.

'What personal reasons? Just then you said if you had known something you wouldn't have come, you wouldn't have volunteered. You said for personal reasons. What's that mean? Am I allowed to know?'

The question seemed to defeat him. He stood in silence for a long time, searching for a way to start. 'Do you remember that dinner in Saint-Valery? When I tracked you down to that hotel?'

'Ah, is that what you did? You made it look like an accident. I remember you made me awfully late. No, perhaps that's not fair: I let myself be late.'

What could she say? That she would have sat there all night breathing the damp sea air? That she had barely heard a thing he had said? That he looked well in candlelight? That she had blissfully unlistened to all his careful words? All his sweet unimportant careful words? All until the blow had struck. Was she expected to explain how hard it was to walk when you feel you have no legs? To smile when your face seems to belong to someone else? How hard to speak when your brain cannot fish a single word from the pit, apart from *Emily, Emily, Emily* - the one word you could not say.

She realised he was speaking, '... the time I spent at that place trying to find out where you were staying, tracking you down.'

'So all that hail fellow, well met, surprise, surprise, was another lie?'

'If you like - an innocent one. It seemed I might never see you again. In my profession that's your first thought now. You meet a chap and almost at once wonder when they will be dead. When you'll be dead yourself. You can't help it. Just the other day, two friends – no, not really friends, just people I flew with. You really can't say you have friends anymore. Shot down over the Channel. You always think they might survive. You're supposed to say that, but you don't believe it. Assumed dead, that's what it says. That's the measure of it, we're all assumed dead. Waiting our turn, you might say. So yes, it was a lie. I was a bit mad: reckless. It's not such a bad state to be in. I tracked you down that afternoon and bribed the chap in the restaurant to keep a table free. There, I've confessed all. Prospects of war make you do things you never would in a million years.'

'I remember you talked a lot. I liked that.'

'I suppose I can say it now: it doesn't matter really. I'm sure you have a different slant on it. Probably forgotten all about it. But I never forgot that evening. I think I'll die remembering it.'

'Don't you think that stuff about the soldier and the girl is a bit old hat? You know, stolen moments, ships that pass in the night, whatever. I can see how you might remember it: a table for two, candlelight, a pretty girl. It makes you forget those back home. I suppose I can say pretty? I was a bit pretty then – well, let's say well-dressed. Would well-dressed do?'

It was a long time before he spoke. He had listened with an odd frown on his face, as if he barely understood. 'Pretty? No, I didn't think of that. When you're bowled over you don't think about pretty, do you? It's a word people use. I never thought about it.'

'Then let's just say a tête-à-tête over the Armagnac with a girl. The dream of every lonely soldier. A friendly pair of eyes. It sounds nice. I bet you didn't mention it when you got home to the wife. What was her name? When you got home to Emily? I bet those were magic moments not to share. I bet that.'

Suddenly she was a child again. It was her nature never really to grow up – she would carry that innocent girl on her back for ever. Too late to ask why she should cry. She may as well ask why she was a girl again. Bitter tears would betray her anyway.

And true enough, he looked away, embarrassed, a slight flush on his face, frowning, searching for words. 'No. I couldn't do that. I didn't tell her anything.'

'And what should I think of that?' She was gulping now, her voice cracking. 'Why do you say couldn't? Why not?'

'I think you know why.'

She could feel his cool stare on her face. She did not look back. 'And how is she, your Emily? What does she say about this French adventure? Or doesn't she know about that either?'

'I haven't seen Emily for ages. Months. I remember now. I remember I told you. About the marriage. I don't know why I felt I ought to tell you that. It was in the air and I've always had this thing about honourable conduct. Yes, I know – that's a bit presumptuous. But I can't keep raking about for motives. I just felt I should explain. And it was the truth. But it didn't happen. No, we didn't marry.' A strange little laugh, as if to put things in the right context, 'The reverse, rather.'

CHAPTER 13

The reverse, rather.

Oscar was turning away, avoiding her face; enormously relieved the door was opening, Albert standing in the frame, looking anxiously at the two of them, sensing the air.

'You told her then? What's she say? It's a chance, Poppy. A chance to get away. You have to take it.' Neither of them spoke. 'Here ... I've been looking out Lucile's papers ... God, somebody say something. What's the matter? Have I done something?'

She saw it all now: Albert had planned all this - had it in mind for weeks. Ever since that visit to the Mairie. Treating her like a child; the shame of his petty duplicity hurt. She should have been angry – furious - but she was not. Set against Oscar standing there, white-faced and unhappy, looking like death itself, fury would have to wait. *The reverse, rather.* What on earth was the reverse of marriage? Not divorce - no time for divorce. What could such a thing be? Some hellish contract of enmity, perhaps: *You I will hate, despise and oppose, until death us do part.* It made so little sense she felt as if the springs of her whole life had been casually unloosed. Gears she believed meshed for good or ill – certainly for ill - suddenly did no such thing.

She watched Albert dropping the limp yellow envelope with her railway pass and ration card in it on the table, changing his mind, and pushing it across to Oscar. 'She's not going to get far with these, you know. Alright, we're cut off here, but that doesn't mean the police are completely stupid. I'm not sure you realise what these chaps are like? They're not locals. We had a couple when it all started, an awful jumped up martinet in glasses and a bloke with a rifle. It's funny, you go your whole life and never get close enough to smell a gun. They smell of sewing machine oil; I never knew that. And, my God, the way they toss them around. You can't help thinking what if it goes off.'

Oscar ignored the envelope, shuffling through things on the table, making space for himself. She'd not noticed that wallet before, the sort of thing old women fumbled with on the bus, cracked brown leather, shiny with use. Had it been there all the time? Surely it wasn't there yesterday. He opened it and pulled out a wad of papers. 'There's a passport here. Swiss. Perfectly valid.' It was her he was talking to, her he was still not quite looking at, the quiet voice unnecessarily patient, as if she had contradicted something. 'Don't go volunteering it whatever you do. So far as we can discover, travel documents are preferred to passports.' How that "we" had leaked into his soul, hinting at numberless faceless people scheming behind it all. For a second she was listening to somebody else altogether. Unpleasant. A new voice, something raw about it; it must be how he sounded when he was at work – she supposed you could call it work.

'If they do ask for a passport, make a fuss looking for it. Now … you're Dutch by birth. That should handle the French accent.'

She smiled at that, thinking of clogs and those white winged hats the women wore. She didn't feel Dutch. He did not smile back, just peeled out another paper from the wallet. 'It's not what you say, it's the accent. We think you'll pass for Dutch, but try not to talk too much. There's a travel pass here for two months ago. Expired. We've mussed it up a bit. Pull it out with the other one if you're asked. It's just for the Department border, not a big deal here. This one's signed by the new Prefect. Forged, but very good. Had to get it done in a rush because they've changed the period of validity.' He was folding them back into the wallet, finally looking at her. His eyes were dreadfully tired. 'If we're lucky, you'll need none of them. The car will be here tomorrow morning – you won't know the driver. Stuart and I will be going with you. The story is, you've accepted a lift to the main railway station. We don't know you. You've a connection for the Geneva train. There's a ticket in there but don't volunteer it, let them ask for it.'

The wallet was in her hand now. She pulled the passport out, getting the feel of it. It was worn, with rubbed edges; border stamps, Evian-les-Bains and Lausanne, dated two year's ago. She was born in Tilburg. God – she didn't even know where Tilburg was! This was all insane. On the back page, her own photograph, signed *Lucile Beyrou*. Oddly, the same defiant look as the old railway pass. Where on earth had they got it? So many intricate preparations, when had all this been done? The papers spread out on the table brought a knot of fear to her stomach. It lurched into her - these things really would happen. It was decided: she was to leave. And as Stuart strolled back into the kitchen, smug with the certainty something had been settled, the feeling of helplessness overwhelmed her.

She knew why people simply took her in hand like this. It was the curse of precocious talent. Only Paul had ever understood she had her own life; not even Albert quite believed that. She had always been the freak at the show: the prize exhibit was always going to be the painter, never the paintings. Too late to say you had grown into yourself; they looked and saw no more than the child they had always feared a little. She tried not to blame Albert – at least he respected her work – but Stuart? Your brother was hard to forgive, shuffling across the room, muttering something to Oscar, shooting her that awkward embarrassed look, as if he were a little boy again. Albert was smoking one of his cigars, tipping his head back and blowing smoke into the air like a train. It was infuriating: he was daring her to notice because he'd stopped smoking in the daytime a while ago. It was depressingly clear they would let her have her discussion, they might even argue the toss this way or that, but in the end it didn't matter a jot. And that cigar said it all: he would not be coming with her.

Stuart was pulling a coat on, holding Oscar's out to him. 'Best get a move on. We're going to be late.'

She had been dismissed. Oscar struggling into his coat, talking now to Albert, 'That boy tramping round the place has snarled things up. We'll have to pull everything forward. Possible, but we won't be popular. It means using the radio. I wanted to avoid that. We'll be at my uncle's place if there's a snag, but there won't be. It shouldn't take all that long. If he's got any eggs I'll bring some back.'

The house seemed to relax with them gone. Albert started carrying tins and packets into the larder. He was making peace. 'They're a nice couple of lads, but I'll be glad when they're off. You too. Don't you fret, I'll be alright. I like it restful, you know that. I'd better get these things out of sight if I'm to have visitors. I've never really taken to Germans. I don't like the way they paint just lately. A bit perverse. Too much thinking in it for my taste. Still, it looks like I'll get the chance to revise my opinions. Or not. We'll see. One consolation, though: I'll get something to eat.'

'Albert, I want to stay here. Don't I have a say in all this? I feel I've been stuffed in a laundry basket … you know … kidnapped. I think Stuart's ashamed of the whole business. But they can't make me go; you neither. I could lay low, keep myself to myself. Come to think of it, if I'm to be Dutch, why can't I be Dutch here? I can't just leave you.'

'There's no choice. With German soldiers here you'd have to hide. How long do you think we can do that? It was bad enough hiding Paul. That was bound to go wrong eventually. I think he realised, poor chap. You know as well as I do we couldn't keep it up. Somebody's going to remember Lucile sooner or later. I know she's got relatives around here. And she wasn't Dutch. Oscar said he would tell you - they've had us taped for months, both of us. There's a setup in the Post Office for steaming letters open; everybody's letters, would you believe it? They'll have read the letters from Pia, God bless her. I hope they liked that stuff about how to make the most of a duck. Trouble is, she never calls you Lucy. And Oscar's right – you're the perfect catch: famous young artist. England's best, a perfect sister of the New France, painting for the glory of New Reich. No, those bastards would give a lot to have you here dancing to their tune. Mind you, there's this to say: when you pop up next week large as life in England it could be a bit awkward. I could be asked how that trick was played. They might get quite insistent.'

'That settles it. I'm staying put. The worst they can do is lock me up. Internment, isn't that the word? It doesn't sound that bad. At least I'd get fed.'

'I wouldn't bet on it. Better do what Oscar wants. It looks like they've got it all worked out. Listen - we can account for you disappearing from here. It's been arranged … just listen. You'll have to keep up with this Lucile thing once you're back home. For a while anyway - maybe a good while. They know who you are right enough - no getting away from that. But it's dear old Poppy the Germans have on one of their endless lists and it's her they want. They don't have the faintest idea who Lucy is. With luck they'll never put two and two together. With luck, I can't see them bothering.'

'I wish people would stop talking about luck.'

'Oscar's sending a message about this now – that's what they're up to. And he wants to speed things up. Says they have to. Things might not be quite as ready as we … they … hoped. But they'll do their best. I'm giving you a letter to take just in case. Oscar isn't keen but I've talked him into it. To the chap I know in Scotland.'

'Scotland, for heaven's sake! Why on earth Scotland? It's miles away.'

'That's rather the point, isn't it? It's the perfect place for Lucile to set up and paint to her heart's content. If they ask me where Poppy's gone, all I know is you've moved on. I'm sure they'll look, but so what?'

'Where in Scotland?'

'Up in the North. Dundee. On the coast. Busy little place. Oscar says there's a submarine base there. They've been bombed, but very little. You'll be safer than anywhere in England. You'll be alright. I've been there myself. It's a strange place ... but they like the French. And the light's good. East Coast light, just you wait – nothing like it. I envy you the light.'

Hours passed and they didn't come back. As the day drew on, everything began to be coloured with a sense of last times. She came to believe that familiar things must be touched, just for the feel of them, for the sake of them. In the afternoon, traces of cigar smoke in odd places were all she found of Albert. She knew well enough he hated goodbyes, calling them little deaths, always managing a wicked smile saying that.

Paul's leather case was where he had left it the day he arrived. She carried it up to her bedroom and pushed a few things inside. Since she could not take everything, she had no appetite to take anything at all. What do you pack when fleeing the enemy, sick with fear? What do you pack when you dread who next will wrench your case open? Somehow, nothing she possessed seemed up to it. She left the case open and went to look at the half-finished canvas in her studio.

The door stuck a little as she pushed at it. There was a chill of abandonment about the place. When was she here last? It seemed like months. This painting was to be her war, spinning things out until the sordid business ended. Ended, it did not matter how, just so long as she could get herself straight. And what did that mean exactly? She thought she had hidden it well enough, even from herself, but Albert knew. She had to get Oscar straight: decide what to do with him, him and his Emily. The Emily who now did not, after all, exist. *The reverse, rather.* There was no resolution there: that solved nothing. So they were not to marry - what was she supposed to make of that? And if he thought the answer was joy unconfined, he was damned well wrong. Not so easy to dispense with somebody who has blighted your days. Not kind, what's more; not with somebody you've painted. Or rather, somebody who sneaked up and got herself painted. Not easy to rid your soul of Emily. She would not be going willingly - and you knew whose fault that was.

"If you want him, why don't you put him out of his misery?" What was the truth of it? Did she want him, now she could have him? Clear enough what Albert thought: that silly suggestive smirk said it all. But he was wrong on that score. Sex hardly came into it with Oscar. In the distant Poppy days, sex had mostly been a bit of a disappointment. Particularly the first. There's always a first, of course. She ought to remember him, but she barely did. All that remained was a few minutes of painful delirium. He'd been a nice looking boy, though. At that College on Cromwell Road. He'd shared her studio for a while, putting his easel in the far corner. She told him the light was bad there. That was what started it, just telling him about the light; because she didn't speak much to anybody then. He'd been surprised, at least that's what he said.

Later in his digs, a tiny room like a furnace with a gas fire roaring away, she remembered a rumpled bed covered with a Paisley shawl. You remember things like that. It was a disappointment, though, that first: a sticky disappointment. Painful, what's more, and the doing of it a little ridiculous. She remembered how she'd laughed and he'd got so cross he'd pushed her off. But you had to admit he'd been saying the most ludicrous things. And the way he looked – like a fish on the bank - you could hardly help laughing. Anyway, she might as well have not been there. He hadn't even looked at her, just gone at it like somebody running for a bus, eyes closed, until it was all over. Sticky stuff everywhere, in her hair, and him kneeling on the floor saying sorry, sorry, sorry. Why do people say sorry so much? Although, really he should have said it, just for the disappointment: that was worth a sorry.

Not that there hadn't been other men and better afternoons; better nights. More than she wanted to remember now. But really better: sometimes better even than life itself. When having this other body sliding into yours seemed all that made sense, seemed all you needed to make life worth enduring. Simply for the pleasure of not thinking; of not having to think at all. Simply for putting an end to the wrestling with things in your head. You didn't even have to think about the stupidity of not thinking. No denying it, there were moments she'd believed that with all her heart. Always knowing it would be different this time.

Only it never was different, it never was; and that was Oscar's fault. Oscar, popping up like a bad penny just when you needed him least, turning it all to a betrayal. It was hard to forgive, because that other delirious body, whoever he was, spending himself, would not have wanted to know she was at that very moment engorged with Oscar. Poor far-away Oscar who didn't even know this chap writhing in her arms. Worse, as she came with someone else's pleasure, always, she knew it was to betray the only person she would ever love.

There, she'd let love off the leash, that's what you get for thinking about sex. But it was the truth of it. She should have said that to Albert. She wanted Oscar because she wanted to be with him, to be near him. And if that was love, then that was what it came to. No wonder they say you fall. Fall, right enough. Into a pit.

CHAPTER 14

Packing was done. She could only wait now. The little case, half empty, stood on its side by the bed. She had not dared pack the gramophone record. It would have to stay here, something she could come back to. If she ever came back. Since this morning, the future seemed to have stopped, changed itself into nothing more than an obscure anxiety. She would play the record just once, lying on her back, swimming in sounds that were bound to break her heart. Walk one last time to the Paradise Garden and remember he had kissed her once. He had kissed her, and down all the forking paths to here, had never kissed her again.

It was long since dark. The little oil lamp on the side table puttered now and then, spurting yellow smoke into the air, a thick, friendly, smell. Mother, a million years ago, always carried her lamp upstairs because Poppy was too small. Ever afterwards this soft light tucked her into bed, speaking of home.

It must have been past midnight when she heard the board in the corridor creak. It always did that. Time was, little Ian would torment them with that in the night, creeping out of his room in pyjamas to frighten them, playing ghosts. But Oscar was not playing ghosts. He came in silently without waiting for her to respond to his timid tap on the door. For a moment he could not place her in the faint light.

'I'm over here, by the window.'

'I thought I'd better go over things with you … to be on the safe side.' Framed in the door like that, hesitating, he sounded absurdly shy. For a second it seemed he would bolt like a schoolboy.

'Are you sure?'

Clearing his throat, searching for the authority that had somehow not come in with him. 'Well, we do need to check through the paperwork. A last check … it's best.'

'I meant are you sure that's why you came?' He was inside now, carefully closing the door behind him to stop her voice carrying into the corridor. Making a meal of fiddling with the catch. She picked up the lamp and carried it across to meet him, almost barring his way. 'I thought perhaps you wanted to finish our conversation. We were interrupted.' She could feel his breathing, as if the stairs had been too much for him, a hint of brandy in the air. The three of them must have shared out the last of the bottle. The farewell toast - men's stuff. Standing there, you could imagine they were almost the same height and for a second she was floating alongside him in the warm waters of *Malapet*. He seemed lost.

'You mean what we were talking about this morning? Was there more to say? I suppose there was. To tell the truth, it was a bit awkward…'

'Why do we always say, "To tell the truth"? It's not as if people are all habitual liars. Of course there is more to say. There is everything to say. You can start with Emily. Tell me that Emily story and I'll kiss you.' He coloured so prettily she could not help laughing. 'Well, *to tell the truth*, isn't that what you're here for? I don't mind, you know. Here.' She put the lamp on the table at the side of the bed, leaned forward, and kissed his cheek, putting her hand behind his head, barely letting her fingers feel the stiffness of his cropped hair. Soft. Softer than she had imagined. How long had she wondered what that felt like? As he moved to find her mouth, she pulled away. 'No, leave the lamp where it is, we can see well enough. There's another chair by the bed. Sit where I can see you. Start at Saint-Valery.'

'It was true, what I said about the engagement. At least, I believed it was true. We drifted into it. I'd known Emily since we were kids. Went to the same school for a while. Used to play together. I'll say this - you can know people too well. What more do you want to know?'

'Look, We're leaving tomorrow. Well, that's what you say. And I'm terrified. I may never see you again; you know that. Wasn't it you talking about the recklessness of war? So don't be silly. And don't ask what more you can say, you've told me nothing at all.'

'The point is there were always three of us. I can see that's not normal now, but I didn't then. Stephen was his name. Nice chap: I got to know him about the same time as Emily, and we all started going about together. Got on fine, the three of us. Did things together: the pictures, concerts, boats on the river, the lot. Now and then it seemed he had his own girl, but they never lasted, so it was usually the three of us. He was called up a bit after me, the two of us in the Air Force. I lost touch with him then for a while. I knew he was flying, but I didn't know what station. Look, do you want to hear all this?'

'Yes. But tell me about Emily.'

'We got engaged, Emily and me. Just after my initial training. You have this feeling – I've got it now – this "best get it done while you can" feeling. It's hard to understand, I suppose, but that's how everything feels when you're on ops. As if you have some deadly disease. I can't describe it. You go out in the street and everything seems sharper. Even the sun. Everything brighter than it should be. And all the time this feeling rotting away in your gut. You can't know.'

'No, you're wrong. I know very well. I've felt like that most of my life. Most painters do. It's to do with wondering whether you can go on. What about Emily?'

'We were to have one of these quick weddings. All arranged with the Padre. I got three days leave – hellish lucky really, you normally get a day. She must have not been expecting me to get so much. Emily I mean. I remember I got a lift from a chap, walked down and thought I'd surprise her. Came round her house, through the garden. Thought she'd be surprised, you see.'

There was the sudden creak of a shutter downstairs. A door banged, slippered feet shuffling across the tiles, then another door. Oscar stopped, startled.

'Go on. It's only Albert. And for heaven's sake stop whispering. It's ridiculous.'

'I remember coming up the lawn. She was sitting there with Stephen. On the grass. They can't have seen me. I was going to call, then I remember thinking something seemed odd, wrong somehow. They weren't talking. They were too close. Then I saw she'd pulled her jumper up, or maybe he had, I don't know. He was kissing her ... you know ... kissing her breasts. He had his back to me. I just stood there. And she had this look on her face: I'd never seen her look like that. I don't know how to explain it, rapture, I suppose. Would that do? And then she opened her eyes and saw me. Looked right at me. Over his shoulder. And she didn't do anything at all. Just closed her eyes and put her arm round his head. Stephen was laughing, he sounded so happy. Then he sort of scooped her up, and her clothes were all flopping down. He carried her inside the house. They had the place to themselves: her parents must have been away. I could hear them laughing upstairs. Both of them. I don't think she was laughing at me. I think she was just happy.'

'And you didn't do anything? You just stood there? Heavens – didn't you feel anything? Didn't you feel jealous?'

'That's just it. I didn't feel anything. Shocked I suppose, but not angry or anything like that. I suppose I felt a bit excited. I could hear them upstairs. The window was wide open. It was horrible, but exciting in a funny sort of way. It was exciting listening. I kept thinking it should be me doing that to her.'

'But later? She must have said something later. If she'd seen you. She must have.'

'I realised she was in love with him. Perhaps she'd always been. It's hard to think about, you see, because he's dead now. I'll never know. He caught it two days after. A dog fight. Flying too low. A Messerschmitt got him. A 109. Shouldn't have really ... we can outpace them ...'

He had stopped, his voice trailing away. The silence in the room was a sort of rebuke: she was shut out; she could never know these things. What it was like to look round a room and know you would not all be there tomorrow. You can't outpace death. She moved a little into the pool of light falling across him, resting a hand on his arm, feeling the dry crease of the cloth and the bone beneath, waiting for him to move. Perhaps he was looking at her.

'Outpace – that's always what they say in the briefings. It's a good word. But Stephen didn't. Or he couldn't. Dead now, either way.'

How could she keep that thought at bay? This was Oscar's world. He lived in it every day. What if Oscar was next? How could she bear that? Half a room gone, then half again. It must surely come to that? His future gone as well. Impenetrable darkness lay there. That, and the certainty she would not be able to bear it. She was made of the wrong stuff.

'Emily blamed me that he died. Said he must have volunteered for the op that day and that was why he was killed. All nonsense of course, it's not like that. But she was beside herself. You feel that way. It passes. And people do say odd things when there's really nothing to say. The point is, you get used to the world making sense, and when it doesn't, there's hell to pay. But to answer your question, yes we talked about me seeing them in the garden. She was pretty cold-blooded about it. Asked the same as you: why did I just stand there? She shouted at me. Screamed why didn't you just come and watch? You should know … we'd never … you know … Emily and me.'

'Made love? You'd never made love? Is that what you're saying? Can't you use the word? I thought soldiers had all the words.'

'Not me. No words at all. Missed out on that. The thing is, I never did with Emily. Not with anybody, if it comes to that. So when she said it was best not, it seemed alright. I think she said she'd been saving me up. Something like that. She laughed saying it, but I don't think it was a joke. It was like that; we never did.'

'Poor girl.'

'I don't see it that way. But we didn't row about that business in the garden. We couldn't. Not with Stephen dead. Dropped the marriage idea, of course. She did say one thing that's stuck with me, though. She said it was more my fault than hers. Said she knew I was bound up with somebody else. She knew she'd never get a proper look in. *Never get a proper look in*, that's what she kept saying. I hadn't realised she knew, but looking back I can see it must have been obvious for ages. I suppose you always kid yourself people don't know. But there you are, she knew alright.'

'Ah. So there's more to be told. Are you going to say who?'

'You know perfectly well.'

'So if it's me that kisses you it'll be alright? I'll get a proper look in.'

'You mustn't laugh at me.'

'Oh, I don't know about that. Look, give me your hand. Don't pull away like that. You can kiss me. No, kiss me here. I have no objection at all. I think it's best you did.'

He took her late in the night, she drowsing almost asleep, comfortable against his side, listening to the hunting owls. There is always a first: strange comfort that she should be Oscar's. It was something to think about as she soothed him back to a sleep as deep as any little death. She'd done her very best for him: you would not want it to be a disappointment, after all. Not after so many wasted days. And strange comfort that he should be her first, she coming quietly, barely disturbing this sweet man, except to whisper his name.

CHAPTER 15

You can make a life out of anything; a sort of life anyway. That's what Dundee had been since she got here. It was the best you could call it – a sort of life. And next time – although God forbid there should be a next time - best not arrive in winter, there being something spiteful about the wind hurling off the vast sprawl of the Tay under the rust of its doomed bridge. And something frightening about the sunset. What was it Albert said? Keep away from sunsets. Right enough, you could lose your mind watching the sun set here.

They had found her a huge studio, the whole of the top floor of two tenements in Peddie Street, opened out into a space big enough for Raphael himself. You could tell it had been a bit rushed, but the place suited well enough. What's more, it had been ready waiting for her. More of Albert's work no doubt. You had to wonder how long he'd been planning all this, keeping it to himself? She could see now why she had landed up in Dundee: the people at the Art College still talked about his visit as if Renoir himself had got off the train. As for Lucy, fame had meant so little lately she had dismissed it. Until, that is, it was pressed back on her, like an old suit no longer a decent fit. It all came back - sycophancy masquerading as kindness; the inexplicable satisfaction people claimed from being near her; the way they sought her company as if something would rub off, even artists - it was ridiculous. Did they never wonder what she felt about it? The claustrophobia of fame – God, she'd forgotten all that.

It was a creeping sort of place, Dundee, filled with war-weary people. Barely a city, just a muddle of tiny houses with sour gardens, bleak stone tenements their fronts blackened with smoke, narrow twisted streets, sullen pends petering out to nothing, paved closes spattered by the drips from washing trailing high above. All ringed by the gaunt bricks of towering mills. Mills everywhere, shaking the pavements, an endless underlying throb to daily life. Dundee was a city of widows, inured to death, half its men gone years ago, whole regiments lost in the mud of the Western Front, bodies past counting. A city of half-men, the ones left over, blind or maimed, the lucky ones, no longer fit for the mill. What can you paint in a city of dead people?

And the answer at first was nothing. For days she slept, speaking to no one, eating only what a silent girl left for her in her sitting room. Twice she ventured outside into a November wind like a razor, only to retreat in despair. When things were settled she would buy some clothes. When she could find a shop, she would buy some clothes. When things were settled she would do something other than sit at the window, watching carts lumber up to Balgay Hill. What in the world had possessed Albert to think she could thrive here? Perhaps when things were settled this sense of dislocation would pass. Until then she would sleep.

It must have been some time in that first week. She remembered it was a Wednesday because nothing good comes of Wednesday. She woke hearing the hunting owls over the Pink House lawns and lay in the blind November dark wondering into what hell she had fallen. There was a stuffy metallic smell in the room. It was too hot in here. When things were settled she would do something about the pipes. The telephone was ringing far away in another room. Even as her brain acknowledged the insistent sound she was filled with unaccountable dread, remembering Wednesday's child was full of woe. She would let it ring on. No point getting up to explain to somebody they had made a mistake. To explain nobody could telephone her here, because her number was unknown: did not exist. It was, they explained, a protection, as much for Albert as for her. Not that she minded; she had no call for a telephone. It had been ringing as she dreamt and she knew now it would not stop. Even if she took her time wearily climbing out of bed she was sure it was going to wait for her. As sure as that the news would be bad.

There was a click as she lifted the receiver, a thin voice already echoing up to her off the table top. 'Poppy, Poppy, my love. Is that you? Thank God.'

You never forget your mother's voice. How long had it been? Years and years. It didn't matter, the voice set her heart lurching.

'Mother. How did you manage this? They said this telephone wouldn't work, that people couldn't telephone here. I'm sorry, I've been so tired with so many things. I've not been here long. But I'm not in a good state. When I get things straight here I was going to find your number and …. I'm sorry … '

She knew why she was saying sorry, fending off what was to come, but it was useless. Mother was not listening, the voice a quiet stream of words drowning her own.

'He's gone, my love. Gone. We've lost him. Stuart's gone.'

Gone where? What did she mean? Too late to ask. Her heart knew well enough what she meant. Her whole life she had been waiting for this.

'Oh Poppy, I got this telegram. He's gone. It says killed in action. I thought they always said lost, it should have said lost, but it says killed. I've got it here. It says deeply regret to inform you killed in action. He's gone. Poppy … Poppy, are you there? Ian explained you don't have a proper number. He got the people in the exchange to do it. Just this time. I told them you'd be asleep but they said let it ring and ring.'

How empty she felt, standing immobile, the heavy receiver cold against her cheek. She felt nothing at all. Bodies must be stronger than you imagine. Even her heart seemed steady. Steady with the chill of it as the words seeped into her, infecting her. At least now it had happened; that's what she thought. At least no need to wait anymore. At least it couldn't happen again, this only happens once. Eventually, reality does replace fear, you have to be thankful for that, even if nothing is ever the same again. She watched herself in the tiny mirror over the table. A pale face staring back, almost a stranger, unmarked by Stuart's death. Brains must be stronger than you imagine. She would never see him again. It seemed days ago she had taken his hand. She would never see him again. It was impossible. All those plans. Stuart. Come to nothing.

'Poppy are you there?'

'Yes Mummy. It doesn't matter about letting it ring. It's just that I was asleep.' How could she sound like this? Who on earth was speaking these calm words? 'Just tell me again what it says. How did it happen? Was he shot down?'

'It doesn't say. That's the cruellest thing. It doesn't say. Just killed. Laura managed to get in touch with Ian. She's been wonderful. He said he'd do his best to find out. You know Ian – he has his contacts, people he knows. But he only telephoned last night. I think it was last night. What time is it Poppy dear?'

'I don't know. Early I think. Do you really want to know? When did you get this telegram? No, it doesn't matter. What did Ian say?'

'He wasn't shot down. It was in France. But Ian says you must have seen him. He says he was there, staying with your

Uncle Albert. Although why you call him that I don't know. He says he was there. Is that right? I don't understand. How can that be? He says he was taking somebody to an airfield. An operation, Ian called it. There was a car - all he can find out is the car was blown up and they were all killed. Poppy? Are you there? I don't know whether you can hear me.' Her voice was breaking. If she started to cry that would be too much to bear. 'Poppy, what do we do about the funeral? Ian says it's impossible. Stuart's got to have a funeral. Poppy, I don't think I can cope with your father gone.'

She slept out the rest of that night lying awkwardly on her back. She had been sure sleep would not come but woke, stiff and cramped, listening to the sounds of the girl making breakfast for her in the kitchen. Stuart was dead: the thought was waiting for her. It must have happened on the way back. After that awful journey to meet the aeroplane. After they'd got her away. And if Stuart, then Oscar. Both of them. Oscar gone. How often had she known him dead? Known it would come to that? She had borne the thought like an unhealed wound ever since Saint-Valery. They had not been running away, not been shot. How can a car be blown up? No, she would not let her mind go there, not near the heat of that. She lay on her back, hollowed out with grief: never touch his hair again, never feel his body on hers, never watch over him asleep, never again wish him well. She heard the door slam shut. The girl had gone, leaving breakfast on the table.

She telephoned Elizabeth later, waiting until a voice raw with hours of crying answered. When they were children and played together, Elizabeth was always the one too old to cry. She was old enough now. She sounded horribly sane, 'Your mother says you saw him. That's what I don't understand.'

'He came to the Pink House. With Oscar. You remember Oscar? It was something to do with an aeroplane dropping things in the woods. Guns, I suppose, but they wouldn't say. Honestly, I don't know. We were both so ill. It was all we could do to find enough to eat.'

'But you saw him? You saw Stuart. What did he say?'

'He talked about you. Getting married I mean. Elizabeth, I'm so dreadfully sorry. He seemed awfully pleased … proud, you know. I just can't believe he's gone. And Mother … she's beside herself.'

Elizabeth had started to weep again, racking sobs like an animal in pain. 'I'm a widow.' Her voice thick and clotted. 'The vicar came with a leaflet about widows. I tore it up.'

Your three minutes are up, caller. Do you want to pay for three more minutes?

'Look, Elizabeth, I'm not good for you now. I'm no good for myself. I can barely think with the shock of getting back … I'm in an awful place. Let me get things settled. I'll telephone, I promise.'

Your three minutes are up, caller. Do you want to pay for three more minutes?

'Stay Poppy, I have to talk to somebody or I'll go completely mad.'

'Yes, Operator, I'll pay. Elizabeth – are you still there? Mother telephoned me this morning. It must have been early - I was asleep. She said it was a car accident but you must know. She said Ian found out what happened. The car they were in blew up. They were all killed … oh, Elizabeth, it's too horrible. How can a car just blow up?'

'Why were they at the Pink House? That's what I don't understand. Why were they there?'

'There was a plan to get us out of France, Albert and me. People bothered we would be made use of, you know, some sort of propaganda, English artists enjoying life in peaceful France … that sort of thing. Nonsense of course. Anyway, you'd never get Albert to leave, you know that.'

'Uncle Albert's not our favourite anymore.' Her voice was suddenly cold. 'It doesn't seem right him stuck there. Not loyal … not with the bombing here. Mum was so angry. You as well. Why were you there?'

'It's not like that. I'll explain when, when … you know … when things have settled. It's complicated. Look, I'd better go.'

'No, don't go - I want to understand. Stuart drove you somewhere so that you could get back home. Is that what happened?'

She knew where this was going. She wanted to scream, *'Oscar's dead, don't you realise? My Oscar is dead.'* Burying the receiver against her clothes, the muffled tinny voice vibrating against her chest, calling, 'Is that what happened? Is that what happened? Why can't you say?'

'That's right, Elizabeth. Stuart was there. Whatever happened must have been after I'd gone. They put me onto a little aeroplane in a field somewhere. Whatever happened must have been on the way back. I don't know where they were going. I don't know anything. I think Ian told Mother the car blew up. Perhaps he said it was blown up - I was too shocked to think about the difference. Perhaps they were shot at. I just don't know. I was bundled into this aeroplane and we were moving before I could even say goodbye.'

'But if he hadn't been taking you …?'

There was something dreadful driving Elizabeth's voice now. If only the call could end. If only she could put the damned receiver down, lie on the bed, sleep. If only she could explain Oscar was dead. 'Things are like that Elizabeth, you can't go back and say "if" – it's no good. War is like that. There was an old priest in the village. …'

'I don't care about your old priest. Don't you dare start talking about old priests. I'm not a child. What I'm saying is if you and Uncle Albert hadn't got yourselves stuck there, Stuart wouldn't have been driving you. That must be right.'

'It's right, but it doesn't make sense. Don't. They're all dead. Stuart's dead – that's all we know. He was my brother ...'

'Your brother! And how often did you see him? He is … was … my husband. My husband. Do you know what that means? I'm a widow - a bloody widow. Do you have the faintest idea what that feels like? No, of course you don't. You've never had a man. You wouldn't know what to do with one. All you know is painting pictures. We were married. Married, do you understand? You don't have the faintest idea, because all you think about is yourself. And I have to be a widow all because you wanted to come home.'

If only she would stop. If only she could take the receiver away. Elizabeth was shouting now, a sick ferocity in her voice, 'It's always been that way with you. People rushing about doing what you want. Everybody looking out for you. And why's that? Because all you do is paint things – you don't know what living is. And you've got everything. More than everything. Money, money, money. You can have whatever you want. It's all just money to you isn't it? We have nothing much, Stuart and me, but it doesn't matter. We're happy … we were happy. Do you even know what that means? You can go to hell …'

She was still shouting as Lucy pressed the bar. A click and silence until something re-engaged and a steady purr established itself.

You don't die of grief; it takes a death to find that out. Grief is just another way of letting death live inside you, waiting for you. Numbing, but not fatal. Paul taught her that much. And don't look for pity in Dundee, death is commonplace in Dundee, people carry it on their backs, are bent with it. At the end of the week she took her grief and picked a way on foot through the sooty half-light to the bank. Inside, a tiny man, lost in a panelled office disapprovingly quizzed her. At first she heard the word amiss. It was an odd word - 'emitted' - made odder by a nasal accent. Yes, she knew the person who had emitted the cheque, knew her well. No, there was nothing she wished to add, it was a personal matter. If she was to have a withdrawing account he must come to the question of her last address. France? That would hardly do. He foresaw problems, difficulties, with France. He would be asked, you see. These were awkward times. She could hardly have been living in France, not so recently, could she? The blankness of her look seemed to disarm him, he was flailing. Was she aware we're at war, albeit not at war with France? Perhaps she had another address? It was hardly a conversation, this monologue with the thin woman sitting opposite him, her legs together, tilted at an angle. Something unnerving about that look. He should watch his step - used to getting her own way, this one. It was hardly a conversation with the solemn face that would not smile whatever you said. A face that looked as if it had never smiled. On the other hand, perhaps she might run away with her cheque, find another bank. It was a vast sum, after all. It was on the desk in front of him, pinned down with his thumb in case it ran away. Money like that must be indulged, or what were banks for in these hard times? It was, after all, merely an eccentricity of address. You wouldn't want to squander too much consideration on that.

He came with her to the door, walking with her under the vast glass dome, hearing her feet clicking on the marble. She did not look back.

Hard to know what they made of her in those first months in the Dundee College of Art. It was not far and she walked, feeling the wind raw on her face, wondering who this person was, striding calmly through the grimy haze of a winter morning. How kind they all were, how eager not to notice her need to be alone. Not to notice the silent catatonic hours she spent in the studio they urged her to treat as her own. What must they have made of her grim silence? One day someone tried her in a kind of stumbling French, testing the last of many desperate hypotheses. That deserved a smile at least; the first since Oscar died. She mumbled a few English words, convincing enough; a kind of apology. After that, they left her alone, thinking she was odd; knowing already that fame merited a little eccentricity.

She sat alone in a vast white space smelling of ancient turpentine, staring at an empty easel, lost in thoughts of Oscar, wondering whether she was quite alive. When she ventured to sit with the others, she would contrive to catch herself in mirrors, watching a calm sad woman with dark eyes talk about painting, wondering who she might be. Each night she would sit in bed, eat a little from her tray, and fall instantly asleep, waking the other side of dreamless anaesthesia to treasure precious seconds of innocence. Until that day's numb realisation fell on her and she knew again Oscar was dead. They were dead, both of them: dead and gone.

It was about that time she began to think of Laura again. With Stuart gone, it was as if she should gather in the remains of the family. Laura the WAAF - that was what Stuart said she was doing. Something to do with photographs that was a secret. And Laura was happy; he had said that as well. A surprise, because, of all of them, she had always been the one who fretted, the anxious one doomed to mother them and resent her role. There was the time when they were children together, Poppy had trapped herself in that cave not so far from the Pink House. The place Albert kept secret to ward off prying eyes, its walls covered with immeasurably ancient paintings. Once lost in there you might never escape. It had been Laura who saved her. She would surely have died, alongside the horned deer and the painted mammoth, if Laura had not waited behind. The others had given up looking; it had been Laura who decided to wait and even she could not explain why. A strange girl, Laura – she simply said she knew in her skin Poppy was alive and that she should wait for her. That it wasn't something you could explain.

She was right: it was beyond explanation. Beyond explanation that morning as well, lying on her back, looking at the frozen blue of a Dundee sky, suddenly consumed with the same obscure certainty. She must wait for Oscar, she knew it in her skin and it overwhelmed her. So that was to be her fate: to stay behind and wait for the dead. She turned in misery sobbing into the pillow. Were these, after all this time, the first tears of grief? How could they be when all she felt was inexplicable consolation? What had consolation to do with it? Oscar was dead. Could tears raise the dead? She sat up, her heart pounding, scared she was falling into a kind of madness, doomed to torment herself indefinitely with hope.

CHAPTER 16

Albert had said he painted that girl - the girl he loved and lost - until he could no longer believe she was dead. Painted her because it was all he could do to save himself. And perhaps that had been true. Death will never visit *Girl with Straw Hat* – she is painfully alive. A little sad perhaps, but no more than that. And that expression? A nostalgic yearning for something you cannot quite see, but only because she looks past you, somewhere else, as if you didn't quite count. But you would like to meet that sweet child, all the same, tease her out of her mood, watch her as she sets her hat down to walk in the garden. Not so very far from paradise, that garden. She was the best of anything Albert ever painted and he knew it. It was why he would never show her. It was why, when it came to it, he had given her to Paul.

For two years she followed the same path. She barely remembered those years now that they were over. Dundee years.

Years with the pivot of her life unhinged. Years without Oscar, when perhaps she was not always sane, her work a hair's breadth from nightmare.

Not long after she started, Paul began to come and watch. He would be there in the vast College studio. She knew when she caught the perfumed scent of a cigarette; sometimes standing at her shoulder, mostly a little distance off so as not to trouble her. On a warm day, when there seemed almost too much light, she would shake the hair from her eyes and glimpse him in the mirror. Long enough to smile that an exception could be made. After all, Paul knew what she was trying to do; she had learned it from him. And he would stop coming when she got it right. When Oscar finally dissolved in paint, he would go away.

It was a consolation, bending your mind day after day to this tiny fragment of war, looking for a way of believing Oscar truly dead, even though, each time, she failed. Two years in which she did nothing else, grateful to be left alone in the white space. Grateful they gave her the time to kill him; *lay him to rest*, wasn't that the phrase? Until the last two paintings - when she knew it was impossible. Until that last day when she saw Paul in his customary place and knew she was always going to fail.

She had stopped then. When she had no more to say. After all, there was a kind of consolation in failing. If she could not paint Oscar out of her mind, she would have to find another place for him to stay. She had done her best for him, you couldn't deny that. You saw some of those first paintings and wanted to look away, frightened. You would look, and wonder how you came still to be alive.

A kind of April anxiety overtook her. The customary fear that she was permanently spent, of course; but something more restless as well. She pined for France. At a certain hour, she would look at her Dundee watch and think of the Pink House slipping gently into the dark. The sun a giant ball, no longer hot, falling behind the grey of Oscar's woods. There would be mist there soon, feathers of white smelling of wet earth. Albert would be lighting the lamp, thinking he would not, after all, eat outside;

thinking of his night's work. Nothing fell into darkness here: the tilt of the earth had somehow unsettled Dundee's light. Nothing could inure you to that.

She had time on her hands now they were finished. Time to spend her days at the window, letting the sunset deceive her. Time to watch the train carry the wooden crates away across the iron bridge. The paintings safely past Kirkaldy now, consigned to Hilary's care. It seemed inevitable that if they were to be shown it would be Hilary to do the showing. A year ago, she had come fluttering into the College like confetti at a spring wedding: prosperous, confident, elegant, full of her new gallery in Edinburgh. As arch as ever, pleased she had tracked "Lucy" down, batting her eyes to add the quotation marks. No, she really couldn't say how. No, it wasn't Albert. Nobody had heard from Albert for years. This dreadful war, it seemed it would never end. Wasn't Albert in France? But of course she would know that. How long ago Saint-Valery seemed. There were rumours he'd been showing in Paris. Stuff not seen before. So he was painting. So he was alive. It was all she knew. She prattled on and on. But what about *Lucile*? What could they possibly do with *Lucile*? How was that to be worked? She could hardly hide behind herself! Although secrets could draw a crowd. Intrigue was in the air. People liked secrets, didn't they? And for the catalogue? Just, *New Work by Lucile Beyrou*. It had a ring to it. No title. Titles have a way of misfiring. There's a fashion for them in London now. But you wouldn't want a title, would you? Not in Edinburgh. How she could talk, this woman, you thinking all the time, *My love is as a fever, longing still*. There's a title for you: a title to take to your grave.

The paintings were gone and she felt bereft afresh of Oscar. Night terrors that had blighted the Bickerstaff years began again. Nightmares filled with Emily. Emily, painted in the German style, without so much as a sitting. How would you title that? Unwonted nude, would that do? The painting she had dared not finish, shamefully abandoned in the dentist's studio along with memories of Otto Dix. Easy enough to see why he popped out.

There had always been something wrong about that man, seducing the wife of his sitter. Shouldn't she feel just a tinge of shame, her nightmares feasting on the cuckolded Dr Koch in his dreadful surgery, complete with syringe. Sleeves rolled up, readied for something, a well-painted sheen of something inexpressible on his face. What was that expression? Anxiety? Fear? Resolve? Resolve to do what, you might ask? What was going on in that German mind of his? Readied for what horror? Not for you, of course, but for somebody. Somebody not even in the picture.

She had never imagined Dundee would hurt her so. That she would be put to painting until there was nothing left for her. Perhaps nothing left of her. The war was ending, and it seemed she was ending with it. Each morning, she would walk from Peddie Street to the College, bringing her nightmares with her. To sit mute and aimless in the white of the echoing studio, feeling the war seep away. It was petering out. It would not be long; that's what everyone said.

Then the letter arrived. For Mlle Lucile Beyrou, addressed care of the Director. Handwritten. It was from Ian - the little brother she never saw. Poor Iggie, no longer playing sandcastles. Buried deeper than she would ever know in some war of his own, some war of endless secrets.

My Dear Lucy

You see I know what to call you.

I had been planning on seeing you. A surprise visit. But it looks impossible after all. I fly to the States at the end of the week. So this must be put in a letter.

I managed to talk to Mother – she always asks about you. She's more reconciled to Stuart now. Awful. Elizabeth as well. There's news there, but I'll leave you to find it out. I *think it would be alright to telephone Mother now. <u>Safe enough</u>, if you know what I mean. See whether you can.*

Here's why I'm writing. Keep this address to yourself. Try to see the chap. I know him slightly. He's a bit of a cold fish, but alright. Don't be too hard on him – we're all at the end of our tether. I suppose you know that. I've written to him – he won't like it much but I'm the senior man, believe it or not!

Go and see him. He'll push back like mad. Just keep at it. Ask him what happened. You should do that.

When will this business be over? We're not there yet.

Dear Poppy, I think of you in your Scottish fastness. It was the best we could do. Take good care of yourself. Much love from your negligent brother,

Ian.

The envelope had a red War Office stamp, dated the day before and initialled in ink. It had been delivered by hand. There was no address on the letterhead: just a single sheet of thick paper. So he knew what to call her. Trust Ian – he could never resist going one better. He surely had more of a hand in all this than she knew. All the same, *keep this address* made no sense, given there wasn't one. It was a pretty feeble joke. And who was the cold fish supposed to be? She had never found out what Ian did with himself. The letter was irritating: too trivial to justify its delivery. Strange. It was only as she impatiently stuffed it back into its envelope that the mystery was solved. Snagging against the folded paper was an old-fashioned Victory Services Club card, engraved *Wing Commander S. P. V. Connor.* Ian had crossed out an address in Holborn and written *5B, Bank Street, Dundee* and a telephone number.

The meeting took a week to arrange. A week of frustration, prevarication, and a growing detestation of the Roedean voice on the telephone. Yes *of course* they knew about her - they had been told she would call. She didn't sound at all pleased about that. You could hardly believe how *busy* they all were – it's not over yet, you know. This immaculate cut glass English voice was not happy in Dundee, that was clear. Patiently explaining, as to a little child, that the Wing Commander was rarely in now. That "now" was a nice touch. Unfair to hate her, given that fobbing off was her job. She had done a fair bit of fobbing herself. They both knew she would win in the end. Well, here's an idea, what about next Tuesday? I know he's in that day, in the morning at least. Oh, that's the VE Day, of course – perhaps you won't be able to manage that? There was childish satisfaction in the voice. But Tuesday was fine for Lucile Beyrou who didn't know what the letters stood for and didn't like to ask. Any day but Saturday - she had an exhibition in Edinburgh this Saturday. But next Tuesday would be perfect.

The flight of stone stairs in Bank Street took some finding, set back and squeezed between buildings on either side. You would walk past and never know it was there. One side of the narrow passageway had been a shoe shop, its plate glass boarded up. It smelled of Dettol and damp. At the top of the stairs, someone had chalked, *Wg Cdr Connor,* on a stone lintel. At least he was Air Force.

It was a tiny room dense with tobacco smoke, two hard chairs on either side of a pine table piled high with files. A man in Air Force uniform standing, his back to her, looking through the window down onto the street below. He turned slowly and managed a reluctant smile, barely enough to acknowledge his own part in the efforts made for them never to meet.

'Not much of a crowd yet. Weather not quite right for street parties is it? Never is in this neck of the woods. Cold place.' He misunderstood her slight frown and was suddenly serious. 'Right, right ... you want to know what I can tell you about your brother. I've got the papers. Not very much, I'm afraid. Really virtually nothing beyond what you know already – a bad do. But take a pew, let's see how we get on.' He sat down and started playing with the tiny cord lacing the edges of a brown manila file. Finally he pulled it open, tilting it slightly in case she caught sight of the contents. A pointless gesture, because it was virtually empty. Just a handful of slips of paper. He sat shuffling them, reading, murmuring to himself, eventually looking up with a bleak expression that set her heart pounding.

'I see your mother was given the news. That's always the dreadful part. I'm very sorry.'

'Can you tell me what happened? Is it in there? I think I have a right to know. It can't surely be a secret now. I can't help thinking if he hadn't been trying to get me out he'd probably be alive.'

There was a long calculating silence. 'I'm not sure why you should think that. Once you start saying for want of a nail, you know … it's not always helpful. I'm sure it's not what he would have thought. Soldiering is a matter of risks, but we evaluate them. People talk about suicidal missions but believe me, it's just loose talk. Honestly.' He paused to turn a page over, letting his fingers run along a paragraph of black typescript. 'They were unlucky. Damned unlucky … excuse me … there's no other way of putting it. A strange business.'

'Is it written there? What happened, I mean. Can you tell me? You needn't worry, I'm perfectly calm. It was a long time ago. I can't say I'm completely over it – perhaps I never will be - but I'm not going to make a fuss. I think your … assistant … I'm afraid I don't know her name … I think she imagined I was coming here to cry.'

Again a ghost of a smile, 'You mustn't mind Cynthia. I can see she was mistaken. Actually, we're pleased you're here. Would you mind if I asked you some questions first? No obligation of course. But your perspective would be a help. Could you do that?'

'There's nothing much to tell. In the end it was all ridiculously uneventful. Nothing at all happened.'

'Oddly enough, it's nearly always that way. Look, start when you left ...' He held up a flimsy sheet of yellowing typescript and peered at it. 'Start the morning you left the house ... Mr Bradley's house. Start at that point.'

'It was morning, but not early. I remember Stuart said we'd look less conspicuous that way. It must have been getting on for ten. A car came to the house but the driver didn't get out. In fact, he didn't even speak to anybody – just sat there. He was French, I think; at least, he looked French. But don't you know all this? It must be in your file there.'

He refused the bait, didn't even glance down, folding the paper back into its file, steepling his hands, fixing a space a few inches above her head, waiting for her to continue.

'I was upset saying goodbye to Albert ... Mr Bradley ... it seemed so irrevocable. I was very upset. I wasn't in a very sensible state. Crying a bit, I think. We got in the car. Oscar in front, Stuart and me in the back.'

'Oscar? That's the chap in charge?'

'Yes, that's right. I remember turning to look at Albert, but he was already going back into the house. He's got a thing about goodbyes. I don't remember very much after that until we were on the main road. I'd got all these papers and things, you see - passes to show when we were stopped and so forth. I kept rehearsing in my mind what I had to do. I was so dreadfully scared I would give the game away. I didn't see how I could lie convincingly, not when my life depended on it. Anyway, I don't sound French. I remember I kept fumbling with the wallet with the papers, things going round and round in my head. I suppose I was in a panic. After a bit I realised we weren't going to be stopped at all. The roads were very quiet. Everywhere seemed deserted. Then I saw there was another car driving behind us. Well, not a car really, more a sort of little van. It looked like a workman's van. It was red.'

'And that was after how long? When you noticed it?'

'The whole thing didn't take more than an hour. I suppose quite soon. Ten minutes, perhaps. I knew it was part of our arrangement because Stuart kept turning round to check it was keeping up.'

'And you weren't stopped at all?'

'No. It was a miracle. Stuart had said we had to go to another Department and the police always stop you. You definitely needed a pass for that. I was terrified I would say the wrong thing. But there was nobody. We slowed down at the little wooden place like a sentry box, but it was empty. About half an hour after that, an aeroplane came right over the top of us just as we turned into a field. Very low. You could hear the engine – a kind of fluttering noise, if you know what I mean. We watched it land in a bumpy sort of way and come back towards us. It seemed to be going almost too fast, swerving about. I remember thinking it was making a dreadful noise and that somebody was bound to hear it. The red van had come into the field behind us and was turning round to face the way out. There was a sort of broken-down gate pulled wide open. Our car had stopped, facing the aeroplane. We all got out.'

'The driver got out as well? You're sure of that?'

'Yes, he went across to the hedge. I think he wanted to … you know. When he came back, he stood with the car door open. I think he lit a cigarette. He didn't seem particularly nervous or anything but he didn't speak. I got the impression he'd done all this before … I don't know why … I just got that impression. Oh, I remember, the engine was running. He left the engine running. Then two people got out of the van, a man and a woman. They went across to the aeroplane and got the door open. The man helped her climb in … well, pushed her really … there were no steps or anything. Then it was my turn. Stuart and Oscar gave me a lift under my arms and I found myself lying on a metal floor. It was awfully hot inside, full of fumes, shaking and throbbing. It was incredibly noisy. Oscar threw my case in after me, but we were already moving, bumping over the grass, with the door at the side still open and shaking about. I remember looking out; the man had opened the doors at the back of the little van and Stuart was standing by the car. He seemed to be shouting. I suppose he wanted to get a move on, that's what it looked like. Oscar was just standing there, staring up at me. Then we bumped right round and the woman started to get the door closed. She seemed to know what to do. The last thing I saw through the door was Oscar walking alongside, still looking up. Then I had to lie down and find something to hang on to because we were bouncing about so horribly over the grass. I'd never been in an aeroplane before.'

'The woman, did she say anything?'

'I think she swore. In French. But the noise was awful. Then she just slumped down and went to sleep. At least, she closed her eyes. That was it.'

She had never told that story before. Never articulated the banal details, not even to herself. It should not have been told in this seedy little Dundee office to a bored man who already knew it and was playing some stupid game of his own. He sat waiting for her to go on, letting the street sounds creep into the room. A crowd was gathering outside, people laughing; there was the morning grind of tram wheels in Reform Street.

'There's nothing more I can tell you. Anyway, you must have it all written down there.'

'I'm sorry – you must think it awfully rude. Before you came we were going over it, trying to get part of the picture straight. You're an eye witness, you see. What you saw helps piece the picture together. You've been more helpful than you realise. Just one more thing. Bear with me. Go back to the woman. She closed the door and you were moving at that point. There are windows. Could you still see out?'

'At first. We swung right round and I could see the two cars through the window on the other side to the door. They all looked tiny. Like toys. Stuart seemed to be waving to somebody. Oscar was still walking, but he stopped when we speeded up. I could see his face looking up. That was the last time I saw him ... I only just realised that ... I'm sorry ... what were you asking?

Yes … the other car, the little van, had started to move towards the gate. Our car, the one we came in, was being turned round. Stuart was half in and half out. I think he was calling to Oscar, but that's just a guess. Then the woman pulled me to get me to sit down.'

'Did the woman mention she could see anything?'

'I don't think so. I mean, it's a long time ago and I was in a terrible state. But you must have asked her … I mean, not you, but somebody. Did she say she saw anything?'

He was picking his words. 'I'm afraid we can't ask her. Now … just a last question. After you took off. We know that was to the South. You would have banked steeply, turned I mean. Did you look down? Could you see anything?'

What did she remember of that? The other woman clutching a stained canvas strap, wrapping it round her wrist in a practised way, looking coolly into Lucy's terrified face. The two of them sprawled across the metal ribs of the floor, hanging on like death. The whole thing tipping like a fairground ride, bright flashes of sunlight spinning along grey walls. An overwhelming desire to vomit burning her throat.

As she shook her head, Connor spread out the tiny sheaf of papers, was leafing through them, looking for something. He pulled it out and read in silence. She may as well not have been there. Finally, he looked up. 'I had reservations about telling you this. I still have reservations. But you appear to have friends in high places.' His smile was not altogether nice. 'Perhaps I should say relatives in high places. I only hope no harm comes of it. I will give you the gist of what we've pieced together. As you say, you were collected - in a Citroen car - at ten eighteen. You travelled in the back. Before you reached the Departmental border you were joined by a Simca van. You passed the border without incident. The two vehicles reached the rendezvous at eleven twenty: a field not far from … no, I'll pass over that, it's not important. The van was carrying a passenger, the woman you refer to. I should explain it was also carrying materiel. At some point a large box or crate must have been transferred from the Simca into the boot of the car. We've been trying to work out exactly when that was done – it's pretty critical information. From your account it must have been directly after you took off. At the side of the airstrip. The box contained an explosive device intended ... no, I'll pass on that as well.'

So that was what happened. An accident. Hearing her sigh, he looked up and she realised his stiffness had been mostly embarrassment. He had been seeing whatever came next in this narrative through her eyes and finding it impossible to continue. He put the paper down. 'There's a lot of detail here. It's how these things are written. They have to be. Details are sometimes ugly, that's how things are. I really think I should spare you ... no, before you say anything ... I'm thinking of the author of this report. Never in a million years would he have imagined it being read by the sister of ... that is, being read by you. I owe something to him on that account, do you see – can you accept what I say?'

'Whatever was in the box blew up. Is that what you're going to tell me? Is that what it says?'

'That's part of it. A rescue was attempted ... extremely risky and certain to fail in the circumstances. Look, I want to pass over this. You have to appreciate those things could be unstable. There's always a risk, but it was particularly great at that time. At the beginning. It was a huge device, capable of derailing a train. There was no possibility anyone could have survived an explosion like that. The car was completely destroyed,'

'It's alright ... I'm not going to badger you for details. I'm just glad I know. I can tell my mother? Although I'm not sure she wants to know now. Perhaps I won't tell her. I'm glad it was quick. You hear people say that, don't you? I never thought I would be saying it. But it's true. If they had to die ... I'm glad it was very quick.'

Why was she in this place? What point was served? Why did Ian think she should hear this wretched story? Did he really imagine this was what she wanted to know? That it was fire, and not some other manner of death? Did he think that mattered at all? He must be mad. Connor saw the look in her face, managing a tired smile as she started to pull her gloves on, registering the tiny scrape as she pushed her chair back. He seemed relieved there were no tears.

He motioned for her to stay a second. 'So far as we can work out, the two vehicles left shortly after you took off. The Citroen went first, turning left onto the road. Almost immediately, the people in the Simca heard a violent explosion. They actually felt the heat of it. When they pulled onto the road there was nothing but a pall of dense smoke. They drove closer and saw the remains of the Citroen completely engulfed in flames. Debris was spread over a considerable area. They ran to the spot. The risk at that point, of course, was discovery. There was nothing to be done. There could have been no survivors. You will want to ask how it could have happened.' She levelled a gaze directly to his eyes, hoping he understood otherwise, but he pressed on, 'And the answer is we don't know. Not exactly. A dozen things are possible. An electrical fault seems likely. It might have been nothing more drastic than a bump in the road.'

He was leaning towards her apologetically. Perhaps he thought that sounded cruel. Perhaps he thought she would have preferred something more substantial than a rutted track to kill her lover. She had already got up, straightening her skirt, looking round to see whether she had brought anything.

'Just a moment more. I was going to explain about the border crossing. Do have a seat for a second. The day of your escape, German troops moved in force into the so-called unoccupied zone. That very day. They called it Operation Anton. It had been planned for some time. We had known it was on the cards - knew the date approximately. There had been concern it would affect your move. But in the event, your repatriation – I mean both of you, because we had planned for Mr Bradley as well – had to be advanced for other reasons.'

'Yes, I know a little about that. In fact the rush was a help. I don't think I could have borne waiting. And if you want me to comment, I can't think why anybody imagined Albert Bradley would leave his house, and his work. Abandon his life, you might say. Obviously, he stayed. And whatever you think of the decision, it was courageous. I'm in a position to know what it cost him.'

For a second he looked startled. 'Be that as it may, we had planned for a later date. Quite a bit later. I can't go into details, but you appreciate this operation had more than one objective.'

'You mean the drop. They kept calling it the drop. It's alright, I know about that. I really didn't believe two stranded painters were that important in the great scheme of things.'

'I'm simply explaining that in all probability we would not have been able to get you out later. German troop movements on the day of your move explain the absence of control points – at least that's our guess. You could say you were lucky …' He was suddenly embarrassed, '… I mean, of course …' He glanced up at the door as someone walked past the frosted glass panel and shifted in his chair, not quite rising. He saw her follow his eyes. 'I'm sorry we don't have anything to offer you. Not even tea.' Pushing the metal tag into its holes, making a fuss of lacing up the file. 'If there were more to tell, I would. It's the fog of war. Perhaps one day, when people on the spot are in a position to talk … Look, your brother was a very brave man. Scant consolation, I know, but believe me when I say it. Will you accept that?'

'Can I ask one question? I don't know whether you can say, but I can't see why not.'

His face had closed on her, leaving the faint smile of farewell behind, readied to say no: to say no, whatever she asked. He was going to keep his secrets for no better reason than a red stamp on a file.

'Questions are hard in this place but I'll do my best. What is it?'

'That report. The one in there. Who wrote it? I mean whoever wrote it must have been there … must have seen. Who wrote it? Can't I know?'

The smile was back. 'Oh, I see. I think you can know that. Perhaps I should have said. It's the only report we have. The chaps in the van reached the scene in a matter of minutes, although, as I said, there was nothing they could do. The senior man there wrote it up. Not long after. Squadron Leader Daure.'

'But that's Oscar's name.'

'You may be right about that. I'll look. Funny name. You know him? Sorry ... of course ... he was in the Bradley house ... you must have met.'

Something odd was happening to the room. She watched Connor pull at the black thread of the laces and impatiently tip papers out, sorting through them. Things seemed to be sliding round her. Far away, she heard the sound of her heart, mixed with another voice, her own, echoing as once Stuart's voice had echoed in the Pink House kitchen. Her face was on fire. The room was on fire. Surely he could see that? She was burning up in front of him.

'Are you alright?' He had glanced at her as she moved to settle things sliding round her feet, stretching out a gloved hand to steady a table that was shifting with her eyes. She must have managed to nod, because he looked down. 'Quite right, it's here: Squadron Leader Oscar Daure. French name I think – that would make sense. Yes, he wrote it.'

CHAPTER 17

She sat for a time on the stone staircase outside Connor's stuffy little room, letting her head fall back against the wall, listening to someone singing; brushing the hair from her forehead to find her face wet with tears. Which was odd, given the singing in her head. Tears were hardly called for. She felt a little drunk. People struggled disapprovingly past her; they were used to tears here, no call to make a meal of it. Two women in uniform, one with a bottle of wine, fell into mock silence, stepping with exaggerated care over her outstretched legs. They looked down, suitably solemn, astonished to find a shining face returning their inspection, innocent dark eyes, wide alight with something that stopped your heart, a trembling smile, radiant with tears.

'Paul was right.'

She felt she should say something to them - it was all she could think of. They deserved a few words, it was the least she could do. Not that they would understand.

One of them looked back as they scampered up the remaining stairs, shouting, 'So he was, love, you never said a truer word there,' dissolving in giggles as the door opened and they fell inside.

A few women were aimlessly standing about in the City Square, unsuitably dressed against the wind. Too few as yet to celebrate any sort of victory, but determined to discover how to go about it. She thought of joining them. Surely there would be music soon. Once whoever was singing in her head stopped, there might be dancing. It seemed an entirely appropriate morning for dancing, although the sun was a little weak. Then again, she felt a little weak herself. She ought to stand alongside these shivering Dundonians; perhaps they would like that. She was perfectly happy to shiver with them. She could tell them Oscar was alive.

She was walking on in a daze, not altogether clear where she was going, her head filled with Connor's idiot talk of Citroens and Simcas; her heart filled with the casual words that had laced up his empty file. Words setting a pulse singing in her brain, *Oscar is alive, Oscar is alive.* What were her paintings to make of that? She had thought him dead; the paintings had never agreed.

She was halfway up Balgay Hill before she stopped to catch her breath, euphoria draining away. It had been a cruel thing thinking him dead. The death that now decorated the walls of that empty gallery in Edinburgh seemed cruel beyond words. No, not decorated: memorialised. Shards of her heart were crushed into those paintings like broken glass. *Bleak* the critics always said; or *dark*: it was always one or the other. She had painted Oscar dead, to contend with the conviction he was alive. That had been cruel. She should have believed her heart. He was alive even now - that was the incredible thing - walking, sleeping, eating, breathing their common air.

She had climbed as far as the Observatory – closed for the duration – and stood looking down across the Tay to the tiny fields of distant Fife, patchworked green under a feeble sun.

Why had he never contacted her? The question chilled her heart. Lucy had been no sort of disguise, not for Oscar. Her passport, passes, papers, letters – everything - he had made them all. He had virtually created her. Lucy was no secret to him. And hardly hidden in this savage place, far from France; not hidden from Oscar. Albert's well-laid plans – all of them – had Oscar at their heart. He knew she would be here before she knew herself. She was not so hard to find: Elizabeth had managed it. Even Hilary. No, she had been hidden in plain sight. And Oscar had not looked.

She walked on blindly down the hill, through the graveyard, threading a way past mossy gravestones, as the truth seeped slowly into her soul. The lottery of war had determined Stuart must die. By that same lottery Oscar had got into the wrong car, perhaps lingered that little too long, watching her leave, wishing her godspeed. By that throw of the dice he had lived and Stuart died.

She was staring at a grave, an ancient stone tablet fallen back against a bank of earth, the writing worn to nothing. How young they were: *Angus, Shipmaster, 26 yrs.* All of them here now: *Gemima 2 yrs+1mo, James, 1yr+7mo, Rose, 5yrs+2mo.* All of them: *And Alice, his beloved wife, 23 yrs.* Having seen her brother die, how could there be a way to her?

She had been walking for hours. There were children on Magdalen Green: girls leaping in and out of a huge skipping rope; boys clambering on the bandstand. Slumped down on the grass, too tired to think, it had gone altogether now, that rapture. Evaporated; and she knew it would never return. All that remained was something small and warm, close to her heart. Oscar was alive and the comfort of that would bring tears for as long as she lived. But he was not alive for her. Knowledge she had battled since she left the City Square flooded inevitably into her head, too tired to keep it at bay, overwhelming her. He was with Emily – that was where he was. The thought had been curled in her brain, waiting, ever since Connor had unlaced his file. He had made his life with Emily, after all. Wounded love perhaps, but enough for him. Enough, now the whole world burned.

There had been two letters waiting for her when she got back that day: May the eighth, 1945. They called it VE Day for Victory in Europe. It was in the newspaper, although Lucy was sure it would never catch on. It sounded vainglorious somehow. Anyway, wars don't end, do they? This one didn't. It just seemed to peter out, leaving everybody exhausted. Who the hell felt victorious? The word was ridiculous. She'd seen the letters lying there when she got in. It seemed like all day she'd been walking - just to get over the shock of things; to get things straight in her head.

After all, it had been a kind of victory that her heart could settle to its normal ache, thinking of far away Oscar, alive as an hour ago. Did he think of her? Did he think of the walk to Paradise Garden at all? Was unknown Poppy still that blight in Emily's life? She stood at the window, watching the last of the rockets spiral from the distant Law. Stood there and knew the answer to all these things.

For weeks now she had yearned for France; for Albert in his Pink House; for the thrum of cicadas through the hot afternoon. The last page of the letter lay on the sofa where she had let it fall. Elizabeth saying she must see Albert before he died. Poor Elizabeth - you need not believe all Albert says. Not lies, of course, simply given to spreading a net of his own, he'd always been that way. But Elizabeth wanted her: that was something, even to say goodbye. It was something to say goodbye. Watching her own reflected face in the dark of the windowpane, remembering a little girl, years ago, dawdling past the doctor's house, barely understanding the pain in her breast. A little girl hearing the scrunch of gravel as a car slipped by, someone waving.

CHAPTER 18

They stood hand in hand, like two children, staring across a wide lawn to a shadowy house of apricot stone. This was the best time to reach the Pink House. Not quite evening, a single star hanging low in a dark blue sky, everywhere still, a cool smell of cut grass blending with the darker scent of night flowers.

The kitchen door had been propped open to give light for somebody to lay the table, the faint chink of cutlery carrying in the still air. Elizabeth let her case fall and pulled at Poppy's arm.

'Wait a minute. This is why I wanted to walk the last bit. I just want to look. It's been so long. Years and years.'

'Pia's back. She went off to stay with her sister before I left. You couldn't blame her, she was in a really bad way. We all were. Nothing to eat at all. It creeps up on you, realising you're going to starve. Worse for her, because there was nothing to cook. She just gave up. I never thought I'd see her again.'

An old woman was stretching across the table pasting the cloth flat with her hand. She seemed shorter. War seemed to have squashed her so that she waddled, lurching from one staging post to the next, holding on to chairs for support. As if aware of their eyes, she shuffled to the edge of the terrace to peer out, calling to someone behind her. A figure sprawled in a deckchair, having trouble getting up.

'You're right, bless my soul. They made it. Right on time. We can see you - you two! What are you doing spying on two old souls? Come and have a drink. God … there must be a god … I never thought I'd see you two again.'

That first meal was a strange affair, nobody quite in their right body. Pia had laid out the food then said it was too damp for her bones outside and she'd eat in the kitchen, she was better off there. Albert stretched out a hand to keep her, but she had already turned away. He glanced awkwardly round the table. 'I've told her she had no choice, but she can't forgive herself. Says she abandoned us. And so she did – I'd have done the same. I hope she gets out of it soon, it's no fun eating on your own.'

A small pile of angry letters from his brother's wife, all delivered at the same time, were stuffed in a drawer upstairs. He had only read some of them but Elizabeth had read them all. As she lay dying, her mother had asked a nurse whether Albert had come home yet. She asked each day. It was almost the last thing she said. He had read one or two. How to explain he thought he was at home already? Too late now to explain anything. How to explain he had not invited these Germans to his table? With her mother dead, Elizabeth had settled for a benign truce, testing the ground, searching for new boundaries.

Not for a minute in London had Poppy felt she was at home. Not for one second in Dundee. She watched the two of them warily sparing, wondering whether this place might be home. Home is where the heart is: that's what they say. She only had that to solve - where was her heart? And for a brief second, as she pondered the thought, something huge loomed over the table like the beat of dark wings and she caught her breath.

Elizabeth suddenly gripped Albert's arm in the old familiar way, immediately drawing back, uncertain of his response, 'What about that letter then? That lawyer - all those red ribbons? We thought you were dead ... well, dying, at least. I must say you chose your moment to say come visiting. Don't you want to know how we managed to get here? I hope you realise trains are quite impossible. Jam-packed of course, but that's only the half of it. What's really caps it all is there's no guarantee you get where you're going. You can end up anywhere and have to feel grateful for it. Thank God Poppy's rich. How I'd like to be rich.'

For a second, Albert was lost for words. Poppy used the tiny silence to tell him about the flight to Madrid. How it was not at all difficult to arrange. And the night train to the border, also not so very hard. Not like the old French night train, of course, but not at all bad; you can't have everything. It had been empty. It seemed nobody wanted to come to France. He laughed at Elizabeth's scandalised complaint that they took a taxi for the final leg. The driver had laughed as well, laughed at the address. Yes, he knew where it was, he even thought he knew the house; at least, he'd heard of it, but it was miles away. It would cost a fortune. So he got his fortune and here they were.

Poppy pushed her plate away, suddenly light-headed with tiredness. 'I put my case in my old room. Is that alright? Pia has put flowers by the bed. A nice thought.'

'What makes you think it was Pia? But you're right - you should be in bed. Things to do tomorrow. Things to get straight. We've to do our bit to sort France out.' Elizabeth was going to say something, but he shook his head. 'All will be explained. I paint at night now ... can't seem to sleep in the dark anymore. You'll not be disturbed. Sleep well.'

As Poppy pulled the door to, he called out, 'There was some woman on the telephone this morning asking for you. Sounded batty to me - a bit desperate. She made the hell of a fuss because it's virtually impossible to get through. She seemed to think I was hiding you under the bed. She's going to try again tomorrow. I wouldn't fret, it sounded like business – with people like that it's always urgent; urgent for them.'

They left him smoking one of his little cigars, looking across the lawn, waiting until it was sufficiently night to work.

When she came down to breakfast the next morning, Elizabeth and Albert were sitting in the kitchen in comfortable silence. In daylight he looked tired, deep lines in the leathery skin of his face, dark shadows under the eyes. He was already smoking. Pia, still too proud to eat with them, standing at his side like a waiter, occasionally flapping at the smoke with a tea towel. Elizabeth looked up and waved her to a place with a piece of bread.

'He's been telling me about life with the Germans. I wish mum had known … because there weren't any. All that time her imagining you two wining and dining with Adolph and his henchmen.'

'But they did come?'

Albert gestured Poppy to sit in the chair next to his own. 'Oh, they came all right. Just like Oscar said they would …' Perhaps he glanced at her as he said the name. She felt his look and her face grew warm, but he went on speaking. 'A few days after you left. A revolting little man, polished from top to bottom. Well, not that little, to tell the truth. Shaped like a toothbrush. Like Kaiser Bill himself, something from the Great War, moustache and all. God knows how they get those boots off. He looked the place over. Looked me over as well. And found us both sadly wanting. He came to a sticky end, I'm glad to report. Perhaps that's for another time.'

She saw the old coffee bowls were on the table, the ones he had thrown himself. She hadn't seen them for years. He must have hidden them somewhere. Funny to be drinking out of them – they must be worth a fortune. She poured coffee into something decorated with a bright red cockerel, leaning over it, breathing the scent of France. 'So they were never billeted here after all?'

'Only for a week or so. Pretty dreadful. Although they did bring food, which was better than nothing. The Kaiser chap was after pictures, it didn't take long to figure that out. Stomping round the place like a dealer. I felt like reminding him there was a war on. In the end he gave me a choice, although his French was so bad I could be wrong. The choice was I sold him what he wanted at his price ...'

He had stopped. Blowing a little smoke into the air. Waiting for her to say something.

'Or what? What was the choice?'

'I don't think he got round to the second bit. A sort of lorry turned up in the courtyard after a couple of days. Soldiers in the back. About twenty, I'd say. Tough looking bunch. They looked uncomfortable and I wasn't going to encourage them to stretch their legs more than necessary. One evening, I made old shiny boots a proposition, man to man you might say. Not a sale. A gift. I would give him a painting. In fact I'd go one better than that, I'd get the Mayor to organise a ceremony. Old France honouring its New Masters, that sort of thing. I must say, I was quite impressive in the circumstances. Mind you, it was possibly the brandy talking.'

'You see, you're doing it now.' Elizabeth was glaring at him. 'Like mum said. Why do you have to make a joke of everything? It's not a joke. They took my Stuart – I'll never forgive them for that. Never. And you don't know what they did to London. Why give the bastard anything if he was going to pay. You just don't understand. Why did you have to be so grovelling?'

'You'll have to tell me what I don't understand. I might surprise you, but now's not the time. You're right about one thing, though: I grovelled as only I can. Didn't your mother tell you there's more than one way to skin a cat? I grovelled away and my German was as pleased as punch. By the time the happy day arrived he seemed to be made of metalwork and shoe polish, a sight to behold. Hands were shaken, painting displayed, photographs taken. They're upstairs, by the way, I'll fetch them if you like. Interminable speeches. The Prefect had a go in German; that made Kaiser wince a bit. I pleaded shyness, or modesty – I can't remember which.'

Of course, she knew what he'd done. She knew it, and felt suddenly cold. Albert was pressing his hand on Elizabeth's arm as if to silence her, staring into her face until she saw something in those watery eyes that made her look down. He had changed with the war and it didn't entirely suit, unhealthy somehow. But it had taken courage, that quixotic revenge.

'It was *Girl with Straw Hat* wasn't it? Why? In heaven's name why? Why do that? It was your best work. *Why*?'

'God, not you as well? You're not going to tell me I don't understand?'

'But the risk.'

'Damn the risk. You know well enough what I was giving them. I did it for Paul and I'd do it again. I was going to let Paul say his piece, that's all. One of these days – oh, we'll all be long dead, I dare say – but one fine day those barbarians are going to look at that painting. They're going to find it and look at it. And they're going to understand what they did.' Realising he was squeezing Elizabeth's arm too hard he let go, attempting an apologetic grin. 'You don't know what we're on about, do you? The point is, they're going to understand, Elizabeth, do you get that? Paul was a painter – one of the best. Painting was all he could do. His work is burnt now, most of it. Burnt or stolen - and there's an irony in that. And yes, I can see painting's not enough when guns are going off. But it's not nothing. I understand that, alright. And so did Paul.'

Thinking how Albert's anger must have seeped into his midnight paintings, she thought of Oscar on those empty Edinburgh walls. But he had parted with his dead girl in the straw hat - and he always said he would never do that. Parted with her and it may well have cost him his life.

'I heard it was in Paris. Somebody told Hilary they saw it there.' She could think of nothing else to say.

'Oh, it's there alright. It was in the German Embassy for a time. I don't know what they call it now. I was rather hoping it would find a home in Berlin but things caught up with my toothbrush chap. I must say the French do have this brutal side to them. He was executed. With his boots still on. Apparently he had rounded up some people in a village not far from here – peasants he used to call them. That was when the Germans were pulling out as fast as they could. It was pretty well all over. Some lads started shooting at them, god knows what with - rook guns I suppose. Anyway, there was a lucky hit and my Prussian chap decided on revenge. Decided on bloodthirsty murder, you could say. Pia told me what he did - it doesn't bear thinking of. They caught up with him a day or two later, stuck in some kind of hellish traffic jam. Dragged him out and hanged him on the spot. But yes, the picture's still in Paris. There's a shortage of galleries in Berlin. I can't say I'm sorry about that.'

He was pushing his chair back as if he needed space to breathe. Hearing his voice thicken, Elizabeth pulled away, irritated there was something behind all this she was not to know. She shot a glance at Poppy and started to speak, but Albert was already standing at the window, an old man, his back to them, bent a little, his shabby grey cardigan heaving as he caught his breath. Pia rescued his cigar from the ash tray and carried it over, holding it out to him in an odd childlike gesture, waiting until he took it from her.

Later that morning a car took Elizabeth for her appointment with the Notaire. Poppy walked across the terrace to look for Albert in his studio. Groups of men with hoes and rakes were working in the flowerbeds. Somebody was slowly trimming the edges of one of the lawns. The sound of sawing was echoing in the woods. In a week or two, the place would look much as it always had. She stood for a second in the doorway, a token hesitation before he waved her in.

'I came to ask whether I could go and look for Paul's things.'

He looked puzzled for a second then his face cleared. 'God, do you remember where we put them? It's an awful thing to say, but I've forgotten. All I remember is we decided on a place and said we should never forget where it was. But I did. Got myself quite upset wandering about in the woods over there, hoping it would come to me. But you remember?'

'I can take you there right this minute. Then you can show me your work. I'm so pleased you're back at it. I wish I was … it's all been knocked out of me. I've had it, you know. Come on, it's just round here. And stop fretting you're losing your mind, I'm always stumbling over things I've hidden away.'

'Perhaps you're losing your mind …'

She grinned back at him and led the way round to the little sunless garden behind the studio. The gardeners had not reached here yet. A weed with tiny flowers, still dripping with dew, had multiplied itself into a carpet of pink bells. Old honeysuckle had woven its way through the wooden slats of the bench. The place smelled abandoned.

'Of course! I remember now. He used to sit here. I never thought.' He grabbed at the bench, dragging it off its plinth. Poppy leaned down and pulled at a stone embedded in the grass. The metal box lay underneath, where they had put it, still wrapped round with tape.

She kneeled and pulled the top off, thinking of that day Paul had arrived in the snow with his tiny suitcase. With the lid off, the tin was a disappointment. The years seemed to have taken the edge off these sacred things. They didn't amount to much: a thin bundle of folded letters, hand-written, barely legible, the purple ink of another age already blurred; a tiny receipt from a paint shop in Marseille, its fold worn to a crack; some official papers, one newer than the rest, over-stamped JUIF across the top; a tiny photograph of a smiling woman leaning out through an open window. On the top, a death certificate: *Ignace Berek, profession agriculteur.* Nothing really: you could burn the lot right now and no one care. It's a mistake to keep things. At the bottom of the tin lay the little Zippo lighter. Albert pulled it out, buffing it against his sleeve.

As she took it from him, kneeling in the damp grass, feeling its weight compacted in her hand, she began to weep. For a moment Albert mistook the sound, turning to take her arm. She was sobbing slowly, a series of rictus jerks shaking her shoulders. He pulled himself onto the bench and sat there, tears starting to his own eyes. It seemed she had a lifetime to weep and he could only wait. Finally, she looked up at him, the hair wet across her face. 'It's not what you think.' She was fumbling for a handkerchief. 'I'd be a fraud to say it. I'm sorry about Paul, I really am. It breaks my heart to think about him. But it's not that. What a hopeless waste this all is. For what?'

But she was a fraud, all the same. She had been touched looking at Paul's pathetic bits and pieces. But no part of that touched her heart. Hearts were for love, she knew that. Knew it too late. That was Poppy's song alright – too late.

'Your Oscar. He came back here, you know, that day. He came back. It's him you're pining for isn't it?'

There was something dreadful about that word. All her life she had yearned for something, longed for something. It was why she painted. Dark paintings if you like, but sometimes there was redemption in them. It was why she lived. But pining? You pine away. It had come to that. Oscar was alive and it was killing her.

She turned her head away, ashamed, mumbling, 'I suppose I thought he was mine. I know it's silly. And now he'll be married off with somebody else. And I never told him … not properly.'

'Nobody ever does - you've not found that out yet? And you grown up? What do you paint for? As for married … where did you get that idea?'

'Nowhere … I'm sure I'm right, though. It seems right … it seems just, you know. None of it would have happened … in a way it was my fault.'

'Fault doesn't come into it. But I'll tell you about that day if it helps. Sit up here off the grass … you'll catch cold. Oscar and another chap – I hadn't seen the other one before - came back here. I remember it was very late. I'd been sitting up feeling sorry for myself. It had been a hell of a day. Suddenly soldiers everywhere. Trucks and tanks churning the fields up, crashing about in the woods. I'd convinced myself you'd all been taken and it would be my turn next. I just sat there waiting. They'd got dreadfully burned hands, both of them. Burned too badly to drive. They'd walked the best part of thirty miles. They didn't know it, of course, but they'd have never got past in a car. They were in a pretty bad way, what with the burns and the strain of walking. Oscar had a fever. I had a hell of a job getting him to lie down. He kept saying he was in charge and he should have been with Stuart only he was too slow. I don't know what he meant – something about holding the cars up. He kept saying he should have done something, that it was all his fault. He was beside himself, saying you would never forgive him. Said he'd wait for you, perhaps you would contact him, but he was sure you never would. I don't think there was anything he could have done. It was bad luck, that's all.'

'I told him I wasn't lucky. You heard me tell him that. I did say it. Oh, Albert, what shall I do? I feel like I've lost him twice over. I think I'm going mad. I can't work and if I can't work I shall go mad. You know that, you're the same.'

He sat silent for a long time only rousing himself to push Paul's things back into the tin. 'May as well bury this lot again ... that'll be best. But you'll keep his lighter, won't you? Try not to lose it. You don't smoke but it'll do for something. I don't know what ... lighting things ...'

He looked so lost she reached out and squeezed his hand. 'No cure for love ... isn't that what they say? You're a bit of a poppet, you know, and I've missed you. Don't fret about me. I'm just dog tired. That journey was pretty terrible. Let's go in. Can I make some coffee for us? Would Pia mind?'

'I've been thinking. I'll look out some canvas for you. I've not been up to your studio for a while but I think it's presentable. Or you could work down here – I remember the days you did that. I sleep in the afternoon so it's quiet here in the day. Set yourself up if you like – there's room for the two of us. Mind you, don't start working at night. It's a bad habit.

CHAPTER 19

A subdued Elizabeth returned as Albert was finishing lunch in the kitchen. She was holding a briefcase. 'Your Notaire chap gave me this. And I mean really gave – not just lent.' She dumped it on the table and slumped down. 'Where's Poppy? And I'll have to talk to Laura – you do know that?'

He poured her a glass of water. 'Did you get anything to eat? Have some cheese. Poppy's upstairs. Asleep I hope. As for Laura, I wish you'd brought her. I'd like to see Laura before I go.'

'Where are you going? She wouldn't leave Caesar. That's the dog. After that dog at the farm who took a shine to you. Remember?'

'Oh I remember him alright. She'll just have to bring him with her. I'd like to see him ... before I go, that is. '

'You're not going anywhere. It's not logical anyway – when you're dead it's too late for trips. You're a fraud, you do know that, a dreadful old fraud. All this broken old man stuff, it just won't wash. No use looking like that, I'm immune. After all morning with that Notaire reading things to me I'm immune. His English is terrible, you do know that? But I got the point in the end. I got the point.' She reached across the table and let her hand rest on his, until he shuffled his feet and looked away, a little embarrassed. 'I did understand what he was on about eventually. What am I supposed to say?'

'Say you'll do it. You'll not believe me, but I'm quite fond of my niece. And you'll look after this place in your way. I don't like to think of strangers. Why not you?'

'Ah, you mean I'm too lazy to change things. This pile of old stones could do with a change.'

'Just say yes.'

'There's conditions. You may be my uncle, but I'm getting to know your ways.'

'Alright, conditions ...'

'I've been thinking ... Stuart's share ... seriously, I want Laura to have it. In her own right. Nothing to do with me. It would have been his ... I want it to be hers. I'll tell you something, if you don't go laughing. The year of that great flood, remember? When you nearly lost your boat. Stuart and I swam out to the old boathouse trying to get a dinghy out. Just two kids enjoying an adventure. That was when I knew Stuart was mine. That day. I've often wondered whether it's always like that. I think he guessed, but I never asked him. Well, he's gone now. When I lost him, I knew I'd never love another man. Nothing dramatic – it just seemed unimaginable ... obvious. And it was true. But I do love Laura. I don't expect the world to care much. Snigger I suppose, but we can put up with that. She doesn't have much, my Laura, that's what I like about her. I'm greedy for things. Not money and that stuff, but life: I'm greedy for life. And she's just the opposite. What's the opposite of greedy? Generous, I suppose; and gentle. She's that.'

'You're surely not asking if I mind. And if you're asking for an opinion, I don't have one. Don't come knocking at my door if you want to know about love. Just tell that Notaire what you want to do. He'll translate it into one of his French mystery plays in five acts. He's good at that. But he's honest.'

'And Poppy? And Ian? What do I do?'

'The same. You decide. You'll never get Ian to live here. Think of something for him. He's swimming in deep waters now, I hear. I miss the sparky little chap. Perhaps Poppy will live here; you wouldn't mind that, would you? She's barely alive at the moment. Pretty well done herself in painting. I've seen it before. But she's not well – go easy with her. Poppy's a fine artist. No, that's backhanded; I could scrape in with her at that. Correction: I think she's a great artist. I've only known one other. She'll never want for money, but don't you bother getting jealous, the point is, part of her heart is here. Let her work here if that's what she wants. I've been praying she realises that's what she wants. My God, I'd give my eye teeth to see what she's done these past couple of years ...' He was suddenly whirling round to a voice from the doorway.

'I've a catalogue in my bag if you want to see ... I'll show you. Sorry, I didn't mean to overhear. You didn't hear me come in.'

'Ah, Poppy, it's you. Did you get some sleep? Didn't see you there, it's getting gloomy in here. Can I make you something to eat?'

'Here's the catalogue - there's a few decent prints. The cover's quite good. Can't have you losing your eye teeth. There are a few prints in the middle. But it was a disaster, that show. Nobody came. I've not got over it yet.'

'Disaster? Why d'you say that?' He was looking puzzled. 'My agent in Paris sent me a review ... well, I asked him for it, if you really must know. Got it yesterday. It didn't sound like a disaster to me. Mind you, I imagine you set the bar high. Martin somebody – do you know a Martin somebody? I can't stand people who write about paintings, but he seemed to like yours. He was mightily impressed – impressed at great length, I might add. I'll look it out for you tomorrow.'

'It must have been Martin Keynes – he said he might be there. But nobody at all came. Absolutely nobody. How else do you describe a disaster?'

'There was something about that. You'd picked a bad date. The uprising in Prague. Didn't you know about it? It had been going on for days. That's where it all started, more or less. It ended that night, ended badly. I suppose people stayed at home to listen on the wireless - that's what he said. But he certainly liked the work. *A lament for a disillusioned generation* - I remember that bit. A pretty phrase, although exactly how you paint a lament defeats me. He said you got something universal out of personal loss, that struck a chord. That's about all I remember. Oh, one thing … he couldn't make sense of the dedication.'

'I didn't know about Prague. I'm ashamed. I should have known about that. But he's wrong about the paintings. I wasn't thinking about the war … I was only thinking about how much things hurt sometimes. That's all.'

'I think he's on to you, by the way. Doubts this Mademoiselle Beyrou who doesn't sign her work. I think he's guessed … he sounds a smart chap.'

'What was the dedication?' They had forgotten Elizabeth. She was leaning over Albert's shoulder, looking at the cover. 'The dedication he didn't make sense of?' She had picked the catalogue up, turning back through the pages. 'Is it in here? What is it? Ah, here it is.'

You had cause to love me; I enter'd you into my heart
Before you would vouchsafe to call for the keys.

Poppy leaned over and took it from her. 'It's from *The Duchess of Malfi*. The quotation's wrong. I changed it.' She smiled at Albert, 'I'll see whether they can change it back.'

He had spread it open at the coloured images in the centre, pushing the booklet back to get the size right. It suddenly seemed very quiet in the kitchen. Outside, the faint rhythmical clink of metal against stone; distant men's voices. 'That woman who phoned.' He was just mumbling, almost to himself. 'She was on about your show. Said somebody was asking for you. Young chap. He'd looked at the catalogue. Apparently he'd kissed her. She didn't sound as if she minded all that much … him kissing her I mean.'

For reasons only she understood, Pia laid dinner for them in the dining room that evening. She had spent the afternoon ironing the damask cloth in her room, spattering it with a little water, until it was stiff and flat. Burnished silver had taken on a soft bloom like glass. She had set the cutlery the French way, forks down, smiling to herself to think how Albert would turn them back. She had brought the candles in her suitcase, wrapped in a copy of *L'Illustration*: advertisements for corsets, a little daring; pictures of the old Maréchal at Montoire. How old he looked. Too old really, for all that; you should leave some things for the young ones. Albert had wanted to eat outside but humoured the old woman, teasing her until she sat to take her coffee with them on the terrace.

Lucy spends a little time each day now down by the big iron gate that has not been closed for a century. Sitting on the low wall, not exactly waiting; more passing the time. If she remembers, she brings a sketchpad, but mostly she forgets. Perhaps she thinks of when the trains arrive: there is that. He will come to her this way. Sometimes she sees him already, sauntering a little, the way he does. Men in blue always saunter, it's their right. With the sun high you would have to shade your eyes to see blue against the shimmer of that road. But if she's lucky, she'll see him first. See him breast the hill. Not exactly waiting.

LUCY

Acknowledgements

Darling Je Vous Aime Beaucoup, lyrics by Anna Sosenko, Warner Chappell Music Inc. The epigraph, *Peindre d'abord une cage* is taken from the poem, *Pour faire le portrait d'un oiseau*, by Jaques Prévert. Robert O. Paxton's book, *Vichy France – Old Guard and New Order*, (1972), W W Norton & Company Inc., for a definitive account of Franco German relations in the war years. *The Oaken Heart* by Margery Allingham, (1941), Michael Joseph Ltd., reprinted, Golden Duck (UK) Ltd., (2011), for a description of life in England during the phoney war. *Hitler's Empire – Nazi Rule in Occupied Europe* by Mark Mazower, (2009), Penguin Books, for the wider canvas. *Divided Loyalties* by Janet Teissier du Cros, (1992), Cannongate Classics; and *Suite Francaise*, by Irène Némirovsky (2004), Vintage Books, for accounts of daily life in wartime France. The biography, *Simenon*, by Pierre Assouline, (1997), Chatto & Windus, for insights into artistic compromise. The film, *Le chagrin et la pitié*, (1969), by Marcel Ophüls for numerous observations on the complexities of collaboration in Vichy France. The author's novel, *The Pink House*, (2013), Lasserrade Press, provides an account of the early days of the characters in this present fiction.

Also by Alan Kennedy published by Lasserrade Press

The Boat in the Bay [ISBN 978-0-9564696-0-1]

Initially, this might be the story Arthur Ransome never got round to writing. But these children do not lead a charmed life. They are given to making mistakes. Their anxieties and fears are more pressing and, although they do their best, their world is not always kind. They must learn that things do not invariably turn out well. Minor mishaps that might happen to anybody slowly become threatening. Trivial decisions have distant and dreadful consequences. Problems that appear solved turn out to be anything but and become the seeds of something altogether out of control. In a terrifying climax, the children eventually discover the secret of the old boat moored in the bay, but at an awful cost. When courage and resourcefulness are spent, there is only luck to draw on, and it is uncertain who will survive.

The Broken Bell [ISBN 978-0-9564696-3-2]

This is the sequel to the *The Boat in the Bay*. It features the same characters in new surroundings. When Uncle Albert arranges a surprise holiday for the children, he imagines he's looking after them, after his own fashion. But things don't always turn out quite the way you expect and before the story ends it is he in need of help. In desperate need, in fact, with his life hanging on a thread and only the children to save him in a frantic race against time. The story leads to a dramatic climax on a remote island in unfriendly seas, cut off from the familiar world. And we learn how an idyllic holiday can go badly wrong. *The Broken Bell* is a book about the acute pains of coming to terms with foreign places and foreign ways. It also gives a first glimpse of Poppy as a painter, hardly aware of her own prodigious talent. The hero, however, is the youngest of them all. Ian never completely understands what is going on, but he saves the day, nonetheless.

The Pink House [ISBN 978-0-9564696-4-9]

This sequel to *The Broken Bell* finds the children growing apart. Poppy must chose between painting and adventure as the others discover a lost lake in a secret valley. The decision to stay behind and begin her first painting changes her life for ever as, too late, she discovers the dreadful consequence of their discovery. Set between the wars, the action is seen through the eyes of children confronting a world they never quite understand. At one level an adventure story, at another, a spellbinding account of a child's first steps in the dark world of art and artists. A book about love and loss and the power of art.

www.lasserradepress.com

www.ingramcontent.com/pod-product-compliance
Lightning Source LLC
Chambersburg PA
CBHW032001170626
46807CB00006B/2599